DOCTOR WHO

THE WATERS OF MARS

Based on the BBC television adventure *The Waters of Mars* by Phil Ford and Russell T Davies

PHIL FORD

1

BBC Books, an imprint of Ebury Publishing
20 Vauxhall Bridge Road
London SW1V 2SA

BBC Books is part of the Penguin Random House group of companies whose addresses can be found at global.penguinrandomhouse.com

Doctor Who is produced in Wales by Bad Wolf with BBC Studios Productions.

Executive Producers: Russell T Davies, Julie Gardner, Jane Tranter, Phil Collinson & Joel Collins

First published by BBC Books in 2023

www.penguin.co.uk

A CIP catalogue record for this book is available from the British Library

ISBN 9781785948213

Typeset in 11.4/14.6pt Adobe Caslon Pro by Jouve (UK), Milton Keynes
Printed and bound in Great Britain by Clays Ltd, Elcograf S.p.A.

The authorised representative in the EEA is Penguin Random House Ireland, Morrison Chambers, 32 Nassau Street, Dublin D02 YH68

Penguin Random House is committed to a sustainable future for our business, our readers and our planet. This book is made from Forest Stewardship Council® certified paper.

Contents

Dedicated in memory of Harold and his tomatoes.

Prologue

They waited. In the cold and the dark.

For measureless centuries they had waited; for millennia, for years counted in the millions. Time for them had no meaning, they did not grow old and die. They did not become restless in their long quiescence. They endured their dormancy with patience.

This dead world that had once been a jewel of life in its small solar system of eight major planets was not their origin – that was lost in the depths of time and space and beyond the oldest of memories. They had travelled through constellations, carried by chunks of rocks; rocks that brought life to some infant worlds, and death to others. Then, as now, they had waited in icy slumber.

Now, in the depths of this lifeless world that had once been home to intelligent and fearsome civilisations, they lingered in suspension, in readiness for the beings that would come to release them. They needed no strategy for the violation and invasion that would follow. In all the universe there was one element on which all flesh biologies depended.

Water.

When the Flesh returned to this dry, dusty world, they would look for water to sustain them, as they must.

And all it would take to begin was one drop.

So, they waited for millions of years. Time for all but the most hidden traces of past civilisation to erode completely under the relentless forces of wind-driven sand and time itself.

Then, finally, the Flesh returned.

Chapter 1

Time and Space

The Doctor wanted time to think. Time and space.

Ironic, really, when a Time Lord ought to have an abundance of both. Except the Doctor knew that, for him, time might finally be running short. The words of a woman he'd met on a London bus – one that had missed its stop and wound up on a dead planet beyond the Scorpion Nebula – still haunted him.

This woman, Carmen (who had been looking forward to getting home and to chops and gravy for tea before the bus had been catapulted across the universe) had psychic powers that had enabled her to see the dangers on that bleak, burning sand-world, before even the Doctor realised they were there. He had got the bus and its passengers back to Earth, but Carmen's last words to him had been not an expression of thanks, but a warning.

Your song is ending.

It is returning through the dark.

He will knock four times.

The Doctor didn't believe that Carmen fully understood what she was saying. But he knew beyond doubt that she *believed* what she was saying.

It wasn't the first time his life had been likened to a song. It was how the Ood referred to their existence. But the inherently peace-loving Ood were so very far from twenty-first-century London in terms of both the temporal phase and the cosmos. Was it possible that Ood Sigma, who had once made a similar warning, had reached across space and time to touch this woman?

He needed space to let his mind process. A safe space without distraction.

Which was why he had come to Mars.

He stood in the open doorway of the TARDIS and took in the vista before him: a flat rocky plain of sand out of which grew a breath-taking range of spiked rock like the hands of some ancient, buried giant; its fingers, ossified by time, clawing at the Martian sky.

The Red Planet.

On its sister world, the blue-white marble 40 million miles away – on a good day – called Earth by its inhabitants, Mars had always been known by its colour, the result of its high iron content. But when Earth's robotic landers touched down and transmitted the first colour pictures of the Martian surface back home they showed a dusty world of butterscotch and yellow. It wasn't, they thought, red at all. The red colour that had drawn the gaze of sky-watchers for millennia was an optical effect of oxidised iron in Mars's thin atmosphere.

Only when humans took their first steps on the planet for real did they understand that the brown-yellow colouring of its remote photography was down to a fault in the digital processing that misjudged Mars's ambient light.

The celebrations of humanity finally leaving its first footprints in the dirt of another world were almost surpassed by the joy in discovering that the dirt really was red.

Well, redd*ish*, the Doctor thought as he closed the TARDIS doors behind him. But people from Earth wouldn't reach Mars for decades yet. For now, he had it to himself, and walked toward the spiky rocks.

He was alone on a planet that had not been home to life of any sort in thousands upon thousands of years, though through the ages it had seen civilisations rise and fall. Its last inhabitants had fled Mars in the grip of a millennia-long winter that was the presage of Mars' ultimate death as its electromagnetic fields dissipated and its atmosphere finally escaped into space.

Mars was a still world, and a silent world.

It struck the Doctor that the only sound in 40 million miles was the soft hiss of oxygen in the helmet of his spacesuit and the gentle scuff of his boots as he crossed the Martian dirt, pebbles and rocks. There were few beings in the universe that were so alone as he, who had lost his entire race. And while he was accustomed to loneliness, he had rarely enjoyed it. The Doctor had always revelled in life; life was an adventure, and what was the point of an adventure if there was no one with whom to share it? Over the years – so many, many years – he'd encountered people who had impressed him with their fearless curiosity, their humanity, their own love of life. But he'd known that eventually he would lose them. All of them, without exception. And sometimes it was his fault.

But now, as he considered Carmen's parting words and tried to unlock their enigma, it seemed right that he should be alone. If this life was coming to its end, then the last thing he wanted was to risk the safety of anyone else. The solitude of Mars would give him time and space to address what might be coming, *returning in the dark*. To prepare for the end of his song.

The Doctor reached the red rocks and found a natural pathway climbing through them. He smiled; every so often the universe offered a helping hand, and the Doctor took it with pleasure. His spacesuit – which he had acquired from the ill-fated Walker expedition to Krop Tor in the 43rd Century – was comparatively lightweight, but it could still make you feel like a gingerbread man on a slow bake if you got overly physical, as you might when climbing a small mountain on Mars.

The pathway gave him an easy winding route to a space between two of the giant's fingers. He had made the climb anticipating, at the end of it, a panoramic view of Martian terrain that would stretch for miles. There would be craters vast and small, dusty plains and possibly long canyons that dropped deep into the planet's crust. What he saw shocked him, confused him, and, in simultaneous beats of his two hearts, both disappointed and overjoyed him at the same time.

There was a base on the Red Planet.

It was made up of five large domes connected by long straight passageways. Off to one side of it was a rocket gantry with a spacecraft pointing up at the sky. More than that, he could see a man in a spacesuit between two of its domes erecting a spindly piece of tech that looked like a weather monitor.

So, what do you know? The Doctor grinned. *There's Life on Mars, after all!*

It wasn't the first time in all the centuries he had travelled with her that the TARDIS had thrown him a curveball. If truth be told, her occasional inaccuracies – whether they were truly her fault or his – was one reason he loved the old girl so much. He had set the TARDIS temporal controls for the late twentieth century, a time when humans had been to the Moon but were a long way off figuring out how they could ever reach Earth's sister world. That way, he had thought, he could be pretty much guaranteed his solitude there. But something had gone wrong it seemed, and here he was sharing the planet with other people after all. And as much as he had sought out that solitude, he felt relieved and comforted in the knowledge that he was not alone. As he watched, the man in the spacesuit attached a sign to the weather monitor – it was two words painted on what looked from the Doctor's vantage point to be an old solar panel: *NO TRESPASSING*.

The Doctor laughed. Inside his helmet it was loud, and welcome. Humans, they loved a joke. Well, most of them did. As for those that didn't, well, their sneering reaction to one could make the joke all the more fun.

He watched the man in the spacesuit return to his base through an airlock, his mood lifted. That was when he felt something press against the fabric of his spacesuit and into his back. Instinct – and experience – told him what it was before he turned round.

A gun.

As he raised his hands and turned, what he hadn't expected was to find it in the hands of what looked like a rough-terrain scooter.

The robot was a little over a metre tall. It had a single electronic eye in the middle of a spherical polymer head that had once probably been white but was now grimy with Martian dust, and two arms with skeletal hands – one of which was currently aiming the gun at him. There was an arrangement of tools around its middle, with a gap that was where the Doctor guessed the gun would fit. A tool for every job, he thought; the gun looked like it would fire a laser beam, doubtless mostly used for cutting geological samples. The robot was dented and scratched and looked home-assembled from other bits of tech. A worker drone in need of a little TLC – not that pointing a gun at people was going to earn it any of that from the Doctor.

When it spoke, diodes around the camera-eye flashed. It said: 'You are under arrest.' Then, almost like it was sniggering, 'Gadget-Gadget.'

The Doctor, his hands in the air, thought, *I hate funny robots.*

Chapter 2

Bowie

Solar flares were messing up communications with Earth again. It was a sporadic pain in the neck for Adelaide Brooke and the rest of her crew: it meant that data transfers got interrupted, and sometimes lost, and had to be sent again; reports got delayed; provision audits got corrupted. (Among the crates parachuted in by the last supply drone flight from Earth had been fifteen packs of sunflower oil when the base had requested insulation foil.) But worst of all was when the waves of solar radiation rolling off the sun washed out personal video calls with the people they had all left behind.

On the screen in Adelaide's cramped quarters, her daughter Emily was saying something about the house they were trying to buy. But Adelaide kept being distracted by Suzie, the sleepy bundle in Emily's arms. She considered herself a disciplined and objective-driven woman, generally without the time or inclination for sentimentality, but the ache to hold her grandchild, to feel her small warm body against her own, was almost unbearable. Suzie was only six months old; Emily hadn't even met her husband when Adelaide had left to head up the mission to Mars . . .

The picture started to break up and Emily's voice kept modulating into an electronic screech. If the flares got so bad the call got scrambled completely there was no guarantee of making another connection. Emily and the baby were lost for a moment in a wave of static, then she was back . . .

'They're going to need another five thousand by—'

The picture fractured and froze, then came back.

Adelaide was getting impatient. 'Talk faster!'

Not that Emily could hear her – the transmission lag between Earth and Mars was a minimum of four and a half minutes.

Then the call imploded in a burst of hissing static like there was a nest of angry snakes behind the monitor; the screen sparkled momentarily with particles of electronic visual noise, then went blank.

'Damn it.' Adelaide sat back in her chair, annoyed and disappointed; she thought about trying for another connection but knew the chances were that, even if she got one, it would end the same way and she'd wind up even more frustrated.

Her comms unit lit up and Ed Gold, her second in command came on the line: 'Captain, we need you in Control.'

Adelaide got at once to her feet. Ed was a

hard-as-nails Australian who'd been brought up in the Northern Territories, for whom Mars was practically a home from home. She had known him for twenty years and personally recommended him for the mission. He was capable and level-headed, and if he said he needed her, she knew he meant it.

'I'm on my way,' said Adelaide, back in command-mode, and immediately out of her quarters, the frustration of the aborted call behind her.

She jogged from the dormitory and recreation dome, the full length of the communicating tunnel to Control. She had turned sixty on Mars; keeping herself fit had always been instinctive but hitting the big six-oh confined to a base where everyone else was her junior by at least ten years (and mostly a lot more), she consciously took every opportunity to exercise. She knew exactly how long it should take her to jog the length of the tunnel; when she reached Control she would check to make sure her time hadn't slipped.

But she forgot all about that when she walked in.

There was a tall, thin man with a spiky tangle of dark hair standing in the middle of Control. He wore a blue suit and training shoes, and his hands were thrust deep in his pockets as he casually studied every instrument, read-out and monitor around him, while the rest of her crew stood watching him in some kind of mute amazement.

Adelaide couldn't blame them. The man wasn't one of them.

He was a stranger. On Mars.

'What the hell . . .?' she breathed.

'Gadget found him out on the surface watching the base.' It was Roman, the young American technician, who had answered; the robot – Gadget – now stood beside him.

The man in the blue suit eyed Roman's gloves that trailed cables connected to his workstation and nodded to himself. 'So you control that robot? Auto-glove response.'

Roman responded by raising one gloved hand, and the robot shifted to the right.

'Gadget-gadget,' it chirped.

'And does it have to keep saying that?' the man in the blue suit asked.

Adelaide wasn't in the mood for games. While the stranger was fixating on the robot, she pulled a pulse pistol from the arms cabinet by the Control entrance and aimed it at his face. 'State your name, rank and intention,' she told him, her voice as cold as the blue pulse of light that would destroy his head if she didn't like his answers.

The stranger frowned at the gun. Then he looked directly at her. 'In order, that would be: The Doctor. Doctor. And, fun.'

To her left, Steffi, her senior technician, a blonde German who Adelaide had never seen rattled by anything in the six years she had known her, clutched the Doctor's orange spacesuit and helmet. 'He was wearing this,' she said. 'I've never seen anything like it. It's certainly not Space Agency issue.'

'We tried to reach Mission Control,' Ed drawled from where he was leaning against the weather monitoring array on the other side of the room, behind the man in the blue suit. 'But with the solar flare activity they're gonna be out of reach for . . .' He glanced up at the electronic clock screen, it showed Mars and Earth side by side, each slowly revolving with their Martian time and the corresponding time at their mission control. 'Ten hours,' he finished.

Mia, a woman in her twenties, shook her head of glossy black hair. 'But if Mission Control knew about him, we'd know about him too.'

'And how come none of our instruments picked up an incoming ship?' demanded Tarak, the base doctor. He had no business in Control – nor did the Russian nurse, Yuri, who stood beside him – and that irritated Adelaide almost as much as the presence of the stranger himself. Tarak had made a good point; all the same . . .

'Everyone, cut the chat,' Adelaide ordered.

The Doctor raised a quizzical finger. 'Does that include me? Because chat is very definitely on my list of things to do. Only, second. First being, gun. Pointed at my head.' He seemed to think about that for half a second and came back: 'Which then puts my head second and gun third. I think.' He nodded to himself like there was a whole super-complicated calculation going on in his head in the space of a second, 'Gun. Head. Chat. Yeah. I hate lists. Anyway! You could hurt someone with that thing,' he advised her like a doctor giving her lifestyle guidance. 'Just put it down.'

Whoever this *Doctor* was, she wasn't being lulled by his bedside manner. Her fingers tightened around the grip of the pulse pistol. 'You'd like that, wouldn't you?'

'Can you find me someone who wouldn't?'

She tried to read him. Some sign in his eyes or his body language to give her a clue what to think about this stranger who had walked into their lives from nowhere on a dead planet.

'Why should I trust you?' she asked him, not dropping the gun's aim by a millimetre.

'Because I give you my word,' he said, fixing Adelaide with his brown eyes. They sparkled with energy and curiosity and joy in so much of what they saw. She didn't think she had ever seen eyes quite like that ever before. But at the same time, she could see sorrow and pain in them. He had seen wonderful things, and terrible things, too. They were all that, and they were old eyes, too.

'Forty million miles from home, my word is all you've got,' he said.

Adelaide lowered the gun and clipped it to her belt. She wanted it close at hand if it turned out she was wrong about him. All the same, she wasn't taking chances: 'Roman, have Gadget keep him covered.'

Roman confirmed and the robot immediately moved closer in on the Doctor.

Gadget-Gadget!

The Doctor winced. 'I know I keep saying this – but does he have to keep saying that?'

'I think it's funny,' Roman defended flatly.

'I hate funny robots.'

Gadget-Gadget!

'There, did anyone laugh? No. Now, whoever put that sign up outside – *No Trespassing*, on a lifeless planet – that's funny.'

Yuri smiled broadly and raised one hand. 'That was me. Thank you.'

'Never mind the sign or the robot, Doctor,' Adelaide cut in. 'What are you doing here?'

The Doctor studied her and shrugged. 'To be honest, I was looking for a bit of peace and quiet. A bit of me-time. You know how it is.'

'A straight answer, please.'

His shoulders dipped from side to side as he seemed to think that through for a moment. 'Well, nothing in space is really straight, now, is it? It's all curved trajectories, elliptical orbits, arcuate horizons—'

Ed sprang in a burst of volatile energy from where he had been resting and placed himself beside Adelaide. 'Mate, just tell us what you're doing on Mars and who put you here! You're with one of the independent operations, right? The Branson Inheritance lot? They've been talking about a Mars shot for years.'

The Doctor pulled his hands out of his pockets for the first time and spread them wide, like an irritated surrender. 'All right, you've got me! I'm an independent! Very much an independent! Believe me, it doesn't get much more independent than me. I've already told you, I'm the Doctor. Who are you?'

He was asking them all, not just the big Australian, and they all looked back at him with as much disbelief as when they first saw him.

'Oh, come on,' said Adelaide. 'We're the first off-world planetary colonists in history. Everyone on Earth knows who we are.'

She watched the stranger take a half-stumbling step backwards. He looked surprised, the way someone might when they had taken a punch they hadn't seen coming. Then, she thought, no, it wasn't surprise it was *shock*.

'You're the *first*? The very first humans living on Mars?'

'Yes,' she told him. 'Of course, we are.'

He looked around him, like he was seeing them all – Ed, Mia, Yuri, Tarak, Roman and herself – for the first time, those brown eyes wide with disturbed awe, 'Then this is . . .'

'*Bowie Base One.*' Adelaide said it together with him. She spoke the words as a casual confirmation.

The Doctor had spoken them with horror.

Chapter 3

Life on Mars

Andy Stone could remember his first harvest. He had told Maggie all about it, more than once.

He said he had been eight years old, and it was a tomato, small but perfectly round and deeply red, that he had plucked from a spindly but leafy tomato plant grown in a pot at the back of his father's greenhouse. One side of the greenhouse was filled with tall, flourishing plants, their limbs already bowing with the weight of ripening tomatoes. The opposite side was a jungle of cucumber plants, aubergines and potted bushes of red and green chillies.

Andy's dad, he had said, had been nursing plants from seeds into bountiful colourful harvests in that big glasshouse in their back garden for as long as he could remember. Not just for the dinner table that Andy shared with his parents and two older brothers, but for neighbours from the surrounding streets. It was an annually anticipated local event when Harold Stone pitched a sign on their front lawn advertising his homegrown produce for sale. He was good at growing stuff, just as his dad had been before him, and the neighbourhood had a taste for his tomatoes, especially.

Harold and his father before him were old-fashioned gardeners who believed in the horticultural benefits of honest-to-goodness fertilisers like that from their household compost heap, made up of almost any kind of organic waste a three-bedroomed house in Coventry could generate. And bags of ripe horse manure from a stable outside the city that Harold carried home in the back of his Ford estate car that would retain the scented memory of the journey for months after.

So, while his father's crops filled the terraces to either side of the greenhouse, Andy's first tomato plant had grown in a pot at the far end: the first horticultural adventure that would germinate a lifetime's interest that would take him around the world and, eventually, off it, to Mars.

Two decades after that first tomato, when Andy had gone home to tell his dad – by then, a widower and almost eighty, but still growing tomatoes and cucumbers for his neighbours – that he was about to become a professor of horticulture, Harold had dismissed the idea that there could be such a thing and, at the same time, seemed to swell with pride that, if indeed there were, his boy was going to be one. And, Andy said that his brothers had told him, when he watched on television the launch of the mission that would take his son all those millions of miles to Mars, Harold had cried tears of pride. Though, by then Harold had known that the doctor's diagnosis that he had kept from Andy would mean he wouldn't live to see him return. Harold had managed just one more season, one more bumper crop for his neighbours.

His brothers had got on the video call together to tell him the news of their dad's passing. The vast distance of space between them, he discovered, shrank to nothing under the weight of grief. And yet, at the same time, he was on another planet, further from his family than any human being had ever been, and every cell in his body had screamed and burned to be with his brothers as Harold's remains were laid next to those of his mother.

That had been a year ago now. Maggie knew he still thought about his dad a lot as they continued their work together to turn the inert Martian regolith into a fertile soil capable of sustaining life – plant and, thereby, human. The biodome project was in many ways at the heart of Bowie Base One: if humans were to successfully colonise Mars, they couldn't rely on drone supply flights from Earth. The New Martians, as they sometimes called themselves, would have to grow their own food.

Maggie Cain had been working with him for two years before the Mars launch, locked away in a laboratory in Iceland running experiments on soil samples brought back by the robot probes that preceded and prepared for the Bowie mission. They had seen so little of other people over those two years that life as part of the Bowie Base crew seemed almost crowded. But, in reality, the two of them still spent most of their time away from the others, working together in the biodome.

This was their world and, after almost a year and a half on Mars, you could say it was a world within a world: a green oasis in a red desert that, according to best estimates, had last seen vegetation more than a million years ago.

Together, Andy and Maggie had brought Mars back to life.

'And we didn't use one bag of horse muck,' Andy was saying as the two of them worked amid the foliage growing in the regenerated Martian soil.

Maggie glanced at him from the instrument in her hand. 'What did you say?'

Andy was standing on the other side of a row of low fig bushes. They hadn't borne fruit yet, but they were great oxygenators. He smiled at her and shook his head. 'Nothing. I was just thinking. Ignore me.'

'Always do,' she joked, going back to the electronic figures on the bio-gauge in her hand, but she knew what he was talking about: they were both proud of what they had achieved here.

She liked Andy. Good thing, really, after the countless weeks they had spent together bent over microscopes and up to their elbows in foul-smelling organic compounds, both in Iceland and here on Mars; otherwise she would have whipped up some kind of toxic goulash from the components of her chem-kit and seen him off a long time ago. He was a big puppy-dog of a man, she'd always thought, and not just because he spent so much of his time digging in dirt. He was shaggy-haired with boundless energy and curiosity; all he really needed was a waggly tail and his tongue hanging out of his mouth. Over their time working together they had come to tell each other pretty much everything. She had been an only child, but Andy was the kind of brother she'd always wanted.

She unclipped the instrument's electrodes from the leaves of the apple tree she was monitoring, and looked round for Andy, but he had disappeared into the greenery around her. Most of the flora they had planted here had been delivered by the supply drones once their work to make the Martian soil viable was complete. They were mature plants and trees kept in stasis during the seven-month journey. The second phase of the biodome project was to monitor the vegetation's photosynthesis, to see how long before the biodome could establish and maintain its own breathable atmosphere. Mature plants would give that process a kick-start, whereas growing from seeds would take forever.

Currently they were all breathing oxygen processed

from the H_2O glacier buried deep under the surface from which Bowie also drew its water.

Water was the essential element in the alchemy of life anywhere in the universe and its discovery here below the Gusev Crater had been the strategic reason for building the base. Millions of years before, the canyons and mountains of Mars had been submerged beneath seas; now, all that remained of those oceans was trapped as ice beneath the surface; only a fraction of the volume of water that had once covered Mars and made it so similar to its sister world, Earth, but still billions of tons of it. Enough to sustain a Bowie Base crew for generations. But the long-term plan for Mars was more ambitious than colonist bases like Bowie. One day astrobiologists like Maggie hoped the Martian surface could be green with vegetation, with a once-again breathable atmosphere.

That work, she knew, would take generations to complete. But it would all have started here with the work they had done side by side in the first biodome. Andrew Stone and Margaret Cain; their names would go down in history.

'Andy?' she called out, moving off from the apple trees.

There were winding footpaths through the plots of trees and bushes, and she followed the one she guessed Andy had most likely taken. The one that led to his pet project that he called Harold's Garden.

'Andy?'

Something twisted in the pit of her stomach.

They both loved the biodome with its warm dampness and the smell of greenery and growth. Andy called it their New Eden, and she had always thought he was right. It was their Garden of Eden; they had created it. It was beautiful and so peaceful. Like a cathedral of flora. But now something felt very wrong about it.

And then she saw him. He was standing in the middle of Harold's Garden with a huge grin on his face. One hand was raised above his head. In it, like it was a prize for achieving World Peace, he held a long bright orange carrot, the fresh Martian dirt still clinging to it.

'Life on Mars,' he proclaimed, his eyes alight with triumph. 'And it's a carrot!'

Maggie felt that brief anxiety fall away, and her own mouth stretch into a smile: 'Your first harvest!'

Harold's Garden was a large vegetable plot. Unlike the trees and other plants in the biodome, everything here had been grown from seed, and in the meticulously hoed rows of reddish Martian soil there were now long perfectly straight rows of cabbages, leeks, potatoes, kale, peas, beans and other veg. They would help make Bowie Base self-sufficient. She knew Andy had been itching to dig up the first of his first Martian crop, but at the same time he had been putting it off, giving the produce all the time it needed to be perfect.

'Hold it right there,' she said, inspired by the

moment, and pulled out the camera she used to photograph her biodome specimens. She snapped Andy and his Martian harvest. 'That carrot is going to be famous.'

'The first veg ever to be pulled out of the soil on Mars,' he marvelled and breathed in its scent, a mixture of sharp, sweet carotene and the musk of damp Martian soil. 'I'm gonna eat the sucker!'

With another big smile he bounded toward the nearby standpipe to wash the carrot clean.

Big puppy!

Maggie shook her head, delighting in Andy's enthusiasm. The First Martian Carrot was a big deal, but she still had her specimen readings to complete. Captain Adelaide didn't check her biodata log every day the way she did with other Bowie departments, but you could bet that the day Maggie was late with her daily readings was the day the base commander would look for them. And Maggie didn't care to be at the business end of one of Adelaide's blistering reprimands.

She clipped the electrodes to one of Andy's cabbages and heard water gush somewhere behind her as he washed off his carrot at the standpipe.

The water would still be icy cold as he rinsed the carrot off. Not surprising after it had been frozen for so many million years, she supposed.

She heard the water stop as he turned off the tap.

She looked round as he straightened up. Beads of water clung to the fibrous orange skin.

'Here it is. The big moment,' she smiled.

He bit into it.

He began to chew, then her monitor beeped, its readings complete, and she turned back to unclip the electrodes.

'So, what's on the menu for tonight, do you reckon?' she asked, crouched down with the vegetables. 'Carrot soup? Carrot cake? Carrot curry?'

Andy didn't answer.

Maggie got up and turned, asking, 'Carrot soufflé? Carrot lasagne?'

Andy was on his knees in the Martian dirt with his back to her. His shoulders were jerking violently. His head snapped backward and forwards, then slumped onto his chest.

He was a merciless joker. Had been ever since their days in isolation in Iceland.

'Stop mucking about,' she told him.

And he stopped. Suddenly. Like some power supply to his body had been turned off. His head remained bent forward, and he was absolutely still. She could hear the sound of trickling water. But the standpipe beside him was turned off. Then she saw the carrot on the ground.

That thing in her stomach shifted again.

Fear.

This didn't feel like he was mucking about. 'Andy. Are you OK?'

His head snapped round towards her.

Maggie's scream shattered the cathedral peace of the biodome.

Chapter 4

November 21st

Adelaide didn't like the way the Doctor was looking at her and her crew; like a real doctor surveying a ward full of patients with bad news to break.

'How long have you been here?' he asked. 'On Mars?'

Adelaide shook her head and looked around the rest of her team in the control room, as if one of them might have any idea where this man had been while they'd been making history. 'Seventeen months,' she said, starting to lose her patience with this strange charade.

The Doctor didn't seem to notice, he was talking to himself. 'Seventeen months? Bowie Base One was established July 1st in 2058. So, this is 2059.' His eyes widened. 'It's 2059! Right now!'

Ed looked across at Steffi who still held the odd-looking orange spacesuit, 'I'd give that a check over if I were you. I reckon there's a glitch in his oxygen feed. That or he's had a bang on the head out there.' He looked back at the Doctor, 'Of course it's 2059!'

The Doctor suddenly slapped his hands to his

temples. 'Oh, my head is so stupid! You're Adelaide Brooke! Captain Adelaide!' He spun round to look at Ed. 'And you're Ed Gold, Deputy Commander.'

Adelaide frowned as he looked around, naming them all: 'Tarak Ital, MD; Nurse Yuri Kerenski; Senior Technician Steffi Ehrlich; Junior Technician Roman Groom; Geologist Mia Bennett.' His eyes rested on Mia for a moment. 'You're only twenty-seven.'

There was sadness in his gaze that clearly made her uncomfortable. 'What? What are you talking about?' Mia demanded.

But Adelaide's patience was in the red now. 'There wasn't a news feed on the planet that didn't carry our biographies before we launched, Doctor. Everyone knows our names.'

'They'll never forget them,' he answered quietly.

Yuri was grinning. 'I can handle being remembered for ever. Imagine my statue. Yuri Kerenski, Hero of Mars!'

The Doctor broke in. 'Today! What is it? The exact date!'

'November 21st,' Adelaide said.

'No,' the Doctor breathed. 'This is the day.'

Adelaide stared at him, 'What day?'

The Doctor wasn't listening. The TARDIS had played tricks on him before, but they had never been quite so brutal.

Today, of all days.

The day they all die.

His mind went back to another day. He had seen the newspaper coverage with different eyes in a different body. It had been a cloudy day in Manhattan, and he'd just bought a hot dog smeared in ketchup and laced with yellow mustard from a place on 8th Avenue. He had found a discarded but neatly folded copy of the *New York Times* on a bench. As he had unfolded the paper, the leaden sky over the city let go the first few drops of rain, they hit the newsprint heavily, like small wet meteors. It seemed in tune with the story:

DISASTER ON MARS
BOWIE BASE ONE DESTROYED
IN NUCLEAR BLAST

There was a picture taken by one of the Mars satellites. It showed the blackened crater that the day before had been the site of the first permanent human outpost on another planet.

There had been no survivors.

Jerking his mind back to the present, the Doctor suppressed a shiver. His spine felt like it had turned to ice, but he didn't want Adelaide or any of the others to get a hint of the frigid horror he was feeling.

He had set the TARDIS controls to bring him to Mars whilst Earth's rocket engineers were still clapping themselves on the back for putting men on the Moon. The TARDIS had been around a century off.

'November 21st, 2059,' he said. In his head the words sounded empty and dead. 'Right. OK. Fine.'

I have to go.

Steffi was looking at him suspiciously. 'Is something wrong?'

Mia's uneasiness had not let up. 'What's so important about my age?'

The Doctor tried to shrug it off. 'Oh, nothing.'

Nothing. There's nothing you can do here.

Then he realised – 'Oh, but you're a couple!'

Mia and Yuri. It was there in their body language. No matter how hard they tried not to let it show.

'Who?' she said. 'Me and him? No way.'

'We just work together,' Yuri backed her up.

But the Doctor wasn't listening to their denials; he was too sad for that. 'No one ever knew.'

'No, we all knew,' Ed said. 'Maybe we can all stop pretending now.'

Emboldened by the revelation, Yuri took Mia's hand in his own big mitt. 'So, it is true,' he grinned. 'There is love on Mars!'

The Doctor couldn't help a smile, despite the tragedy that was to come.

The tragedy he knew he could do nothing to stop.

'Don't tell me,' he said, 'the captain doesn't approve of couples in her crew.'

It was written all over Adelaide's face. 'I decided it was more easily contained if nothing was said. So thank you for that, Doctor.' Adelaide turned to the lovers. 'As for you two, from now on I'm allocating you separate shifts in different domes.'

Yuri nodded as Mia pulled her hand from his, but both stayed smiling.

'They said you were severe! But blimey!' The Doctor swaggered up to her, marvelling. 'Adelaide Brooke! Captain Adelaide! The Legend!'

'What are you, my fan club?'

'Well, I suppose, in a way. I can tell you for a fact, Suzie will be so proud of you.'

'Leave my family out of this,' she snapped.

'Yeah. Point taken.' The Doctor pushed his hands back in his pockets and shrugged with contrition. 'Not fair. Sorry.'

He took in the room, the crew of Bowie Base One. Just a matter of hours before they would all die. The log data, automatically transmitted to Mission Control, would show that in the last few seconds of its existence the base had engaged its highest emergency protocol and the nuclear reactor that powered the base had gone critical and blown. There had been a countdown to self-destruct. The log data didn't give any clues why. And to the Doctor it didn't matter.

'I should go,' he said. 'I really should go. I'm sorry, all of you. I'm so sorry. But it's one of those very rare times when I've got no choice. No choice at all.'

He shook Ed's hand, then Yuri's and Mia's. Even

Roman's gloved hand, which made Gadget's hand go up and down too. The crew stared at him, confused and bewildered as he went round the room. 'It's been an honour. Seriously. A very great honour to meet you all. The Martian Pioneers. Thank you. Thank you all.'

He went to shake Adelaide's hand. But stopped. Something wasn't quite right.

'Hold on. There should be two more. Bowie Base One has a crew of nine, not seven. Maggie Cain and Andrew Stone.'

'They're working in the biodome,' Ed told him.

'Astrobiologist and professor of horticulture, where else would they be? Of course. Sorry. My head is a shed. Garden shed.'

'You want to meet them?' Ed asked; he was already reaching for the mic on a nearby console: 'Control to the biodome. Maggie, do you copy?'

There was no answer. The Doctor listened to the empty silence at the other end of the call and told himself there was nothing unusual in it. Andy and Maggie might be busy pruning, or planting, or whatever it was the two of them did in the biodome. The silence didn't have to mean that something was wrong. That whatever happened to Bowie Base One was starting. In any case, he had to be going.

Ed was saying, 'Maggie? Andy?'

There was a low, watery growl over the control room speakers.

The Doctor saw the Bowie crew look at each other. The air in Control suddenly felt heavy, pressing down on them all.

'What was that?' It was Mia, speaking for all of them.

The sound came again: ugly and feral and primeval. If there was intelligence in it, it was a low bestial cunning. It was like a half-drowned man snarling with unrelenting hate, his throat and lungs flooded, refusing to die.

The Doctor felt his blood run cold. It wasn't just the drowned voice coming over the control room speakers, it was his own helplessness. Whatever they were hearing, whatever was happening in the biodome, there was nothing he could do about it. Not this time.

'Really should go,' he murmured.

'Ed,' barked Adelaide, 'show me the biodome. Now.'

Ed worked at the communications console, but its monitor screen just showed static. 'The internal cameras are down,' he said.

'Get me an exterior shot.'

A camera somewhere among the Bowie Base domes came online. Everybody in the room watched as it swung round to find the biodome. Unlike the other domes, this one was constructed with hexagons of some kind of toughened transparent polymer designed to make the most of the light during the Martian day to boost plant growth. But night had fallen now; the biodome was lit by lamps. And as they watched, one by one, the lamps were going out.

Tarak was at Ed's shoulder, transfixed by the darkening transparent dome. 'What's going on over there?'

Adelaide turned away from the screen, any worry compressed into business-like competence: 'I'm going over.'

The Doctor took his spacesuit from Steffi. 'Right. Well, it really is time I was gone.'

'You're not going anywhere, Doctor, except with me.'

The Doctor looked at Adelaide. Inside it felt like his hearts were breaking. 'I'm sorry, Captain Adelaide. I'd love to help. But I'm leaving. Right now.'

'Steffi, take his suit and lock it up,' Adelaide commanded. 'Whatever's going on, it started when you turned up. So you're coming with me over to the biodome.'

Steffi did as she was told and took the suit back from the Doctor.

Despite himself, despite what he knew he was bound to do by the Laws of Time and the most sacred commandments of his lost people, the Doctor let her take it.

Chapter 5

Garden of Horrors

'*No one ever knew*,' Adelaide said as they made their way from Control to the biodome. The Doctor pretended not to know what she was talking about, but she wasn't letting go. 'It's what you said about Mia and Yuri. You weren't talking about us – my crew – not realising they were together. It was past tense. What does that mean?'

They were walking through a long tunnel. It wasn't unlike a train tunnel on the London Underground – dark, lit intermittently by lamps that plunged more space into shadow than they illuminated – except that it was perfectly straight. He had encountered more than grim-tempered commuters in those tunnels under London in the past, and to him it seemed that one tunnel was much the same as any other – they rarely led anywhere good. Coming up behind him and Adelaide were Tarak and Yuri. Behind them trundled Gadget, but at least the robot was keeping quiet for now.

'Well, Doctor?' Adelaide prompted when he didn't answer.

He shrugged with a casualness he didn't feel. 'I just open my mouth. Words come out. They don't always make a lot of sense.'

'Telling me,' said Tarak.

The Doctor glanced back over his shoulder and shone the torchlight he was carrying up at Tarak's face, so it lit him momentarily like a Hallowe'en lantern. 'Thank you, doctor.'

'Any time, Doctor,' Tarak came back testily.

And from behind him: *Gadget-Gadget!*

The Doctor rolled his eyes. 'I hate robots, did I say?'

Roman's voice came through their personal comms in the tunnel: 'Whatever, Doctor. What's wrong with robots, anyway?'

The Doctor played the beam of his torch over the tunnel walls and roof, not really knowing what he was expecting to find but knowing it might not be healthy for any of them. 'It's not the robots,' he explained. 'It's the humans dressing them up, calling them names like Robbie, or Huey, Dewey and Louie and giving them silly voices.'

Gadget-Gadget!

'It's like you're reducing them.'

Yuri barked an abrupt laugh. 'A friend of mine, she dressed her domestic bot like a dog.'

'Ah. Well. Dogs. That's different,' said the Doctor.

Whatever the Doctor had to say about Gadget, Roman was clearly proud of him: 'I made Gadget from spare parts for the construction drones that built Bowie Base. Now, that is impressive tech—'

Adelaide cut in: 'That's enough. This channel is for essential communications only.'

Roman went quiet, and the four of them, followed by Gadget, carried on along the tunnel in silence. The Doctor continued to spray torchlight either side and above them, but he kept finding his eyes drawn back to Adelaide. She was tall and slim with blonde hair tied back. High cheekbones. She was a woman who would stand out in a crowd. *Striking* was probably the word. But not just because of how she looked; you could sense the strength in her; it was like she was built from platinum. *Graceful steel*, he thought.

'You know, I've read all the stuff about you, Adelaide. But the one thing they never said was . . . was it worth it?'

Adelaide kept her own torchlight focused on the way ahead, didn't even look at him. 'The mission? We've proved beyond doubt that humans can live off-world for extended periods.'

'No, all of it,' he said. 'They say you sacrificed just about everything, devoted your whole life to getting here. So . . . *was* it worth it?'

As the beam of light burrowed into the shadows ahead of them, Adelaide kept her eyes forward. She didn't look at the Doctor, and she never looked back.

There was no point. The past was another world, literally, and she had left it behind along with the wreckage of her ruined marriage that had been unable to withstand the pressures of her ambition and drive to reach Mars, and the daughter that had been the one golden prize of that relationship. Her daughter and now her granddaughter.

But, Adelaide told herself, she would see Emily again one day, and hold little Suzie for the first time.

She stopped for a moment, catching her breath, and turned toward the Doctor. 'You ask, was it worth it – knowing what it's been like on Earth for the last forty years?'

The Doctor nodded slowly.

'Pandemic, war, climate crisis, drought and famine. The Oil Apocalypse. We were facing extinction. Then . . .' Adelaide closed her eyes for a few moments. 'Then, to escape, to fly above all that. To give humanity new hope, on a world with no pollution. No footprints. Where the only straight line is the sunlight . . . Yes, Doctor, it was worth it.'

His face lit up with joy as he smiled at her. 'Oh, that's the Adelaide Brooke I always wanted to meet,' he said. 'The woman with starlight in her soul.'

Adelaide looked at him with her own kind of wonder. 'You're a strange man, Doctor, whoever you are.'

'Thank you,' he said and followed her as she moved off into the gloom of the tunnel again.

It was only a few steps before their torch beams found a shape on the floor.

'What's that?' Adelaide was already running towards it as the words left her. The Doctor and the others were close on her heels.

It was Maggie.

'Don't touch her!' the Doctor snapped.

The body was lying face down, both hands were clenched into fists. Adelaide crouched over her. 'Maggie? Can you hear me?'

Maggie didn't respond, didn't move.

The Doctor concentrated his torch beam beyond the body. About a hundred metres further on was an airlock. 'Does that lead to the biodome?'

'Yes,' Adelaide told him.

Tarak and Yuri had each snapped on a pair of surgical gloves, and now gently turned Maggie over. Her face was lifeless, there was a cut on her forehead. Tarak set his fingers to the side of her neck.

'Well?' said Adelaide.

Tarak nodded. 'Pulse is very thready, but she's alive.' He gently touched her cheek. 'Maggie? It's Tarak.'

Yuri had opened the medical kit that was slung over his shoulder and was fixing up the head wound. 'Don't worry, Maggie,' he was saying, 'we'll look after you now.'

Adelaide watched the medics, then looked at the Doctor: 'In seventeen months the biggest medical emergency we've had was a broken finger. What happened here?'

Tarak opened Maggie's eyes and checked them with a small torch. Her pupils reacted to the light, contracting tightly. But her eyes looked glassy and lifeless.

'The question is,' the Doctor mused, 'if she was out here with Andy Stone, why didn't he help her?'

Adelaide didn't answer.

'We need to get her to sickbay,' Tarak said, shifting his gaze to Yuri.

'No problem,' said the big Russian and he lifted her up easily in his arms. 'Take it easy, sleepyhead,' he whispered to her and strode into the semi-darkness back the way they had come.

Adelaide spoke into her comms and told Ed that they had found Maggie unconscious and Yuri was taking her to the medical facility. 'I want her kept under observation in isolation until we find out what's going on here.'

'What about Andy?' he asked.

'We're going into the biodome to look for him.'

'Wait there. I'm coming.'

She stiffened with controlled anger, never one to take kindly to masculine suggestions she might need help. 'Maintain your post,' she told the Australian sharply.

'Captain, you're going to need me,' Ed persisted. 'If Andy had anything to do with what happened to

Maggie, he's clearly had some sort of breakdown. He has to be considered dangerous. I'm on my way!'

'Gold, if you set one foot outside of Control, I will put you on a charge!'

In the control room, Steffi looked up from her work at the tech console, running a recording of the strange noise from the biodome through audio analysis software. She watched Ed's hands close into fists, the tendons in his arms tightening like bridge cables in a hurricane. They both knew Adelaide meant it. The question was whether Ed would go rogue any way.

'Fine,' he said in the end, and softened his voice. 'Just take care, Captain. OK?'

Adelaide's voice punctured his concern. 'I'll report in when we've located Stone. Out.'

Steffi pretended to be too engrossed in her work to have noticed the exchange, but she could feel Ed simmer.

As Adelaide put the comms unit away, the Doctor raised an eyebrow. 'When they put you in command, they really put you in command, didn't they?'

'Command is non-negotiable,' she said simply, and paced on towards the airlock.

The Doctor and Tarak exchanged a glance.

'She told me once she had spent a lifetime preparing for this,' Tarak said quietly as they followed her. 'Our lives were her responsibility and the only way she could fulfil that was to do things the way she believed was right.'

'She's certainly a model of self-confidence.'

Tarak smiled. 'Captain Brooke's a remarkable woman.'

The Doctor nodded with a mixture of admiration and sadness; she certainly was, and she would die with the rest of them just the same.

They caught up with Adelaide at the airlock where she was typing in the passcode. Heavy seals disengaged and the door opened for them. They left Gadget at the airlock door and stepped inside. The Doctor guessed that the transparent hexagons of the biodome's construction that he'd seen on the monitor screen were less resistant to micro-meteor strikes than the rest of the base: hence the airlock, in case of the worst. They had come through another airlock as they entered the tunnel; decompression of the whole base would have been catastrophic, whereas if they only lost the biodome, they would measure the cost in plant-life alone, not human.

But when the air pressures equalised in the airlock, and Adelaide opened the second door into the biodome on the other side, the torchlight showed him how even that loss would be a tragedy. The biodome was a jungle of greenery. The scent of it was wonderfully dizzying.

'Wow!' the Doctor gasped. 'This is impressive! Is that birdsong? Are there birds, too?'

'And insects,' Adelaide replied. 'The biodome is exactly that. A fully contained ecosystem.'

Tarak said, 'It's going to be hard to find Andy by torchlight if he's unconscious in here.'

The Doctor spotted a control plinth near the airlock door and swept his sonic screwdriver over it. 'And there was light,' he grinned as the lamps came back on and the biodome was fully illuminated with soft, white light.

'Whatever was that device?' asked Adelaide.

'Just a screwdriver,' he said spinning the implement in the air, catching it and pocketing it. 'I never leave home without it.'

'Are you the Doctor or the Janitor?'

'Sounds like me, the cosmic maintenance man. Always fixing up the universe when it starts falling apart. I should wear a cap.'

Then the comms was live again. It was Steffi.

'Captain?' She sounded shaken. 'That sound we heard. It's Andy's voiceprint, Captain. It's Andy.'

'What?' Tarak gasped.

The Doctor saw the confused disbelief on the medic's face and watched Adelaide's jaw tighten as she absorbed the information from Control. 'Is that confirmed?' she asked.

Steffi's voice came back: she had run the recording

through every comparative test she could and it was a positive voice-print match. There was no question.

The Doctor had a strange sense of disembodied observation. The snarl he had heard over the speaker in the control room had not been human. He was just as positive of that as Steffi was of her test results. He knew it was the beginning of whatever led to the destruction of Bowie Base One. But he was powerless to do anything about it.

He should never have been there.

And he didn't think whatever was waiting for them here would be anything that even Adelaide could be prepared for.

But all he could do was bear witness

'Thank you, Steffi. Stand by,' Adelaide said, and put the comms unit away. Whatever might have been going on in her head, the Doctor thought, on the surface she was utterly unfazed and business-as-usual. His admiration made him feel all the more sorry for her, and for the other innocent victims of whatever was to come.

'Tarak, check External Door South. Ensure it's intact. If you see any signs of Andy, don't engage. We have no idea of his state of mind. Contact me immediately. He might be dangerous.'

Tarak absorbed her warning and nodded. 'Yes, Captain.'

The Doctor watched him make his way along a pathway through the vegetation.

Adelaide indicated another route, 'We go this way.'

He followed close on her heels. Whatever was waiting for them in the biodome, it couldn't stop him marvelling at the result of Andy and Maggie's work. 'Andy and Maggie. They did all this in seventeen months?'

'The first few months were intensive treatments of the Martian soil. It had been entirely dead for millions of years. Maggie and Andy introduced new micro-organisms to regenerate it. Long-term, it's the first stage in terraforming the whole planet.'

'I sort of like it red. But I've always been a fan of human ingenuity. When they're not blowing stuff up, anyway.'

She stopped abruptly and looked at him. 'Are you trying to distract me, Doctor?'

'Distract you?'

'All this interest in the biodome. Do you know what's happened to Andy Stone?'

'No,' he protested. 'Not at all. You have my word. I promise. But what he and Maggie have done here is amazing. And important. What you're all doing here is so important.'

He felt her eyes gauging him for a long moment, then she was on the move again. 'Oh, the imperative here was Christmas dinner,' she was saying. 'Our first one came out of a packet. This year they're all banking on the real thing.'

'What? Including sprouts?'

She stopped again: 'Oh, I hope not.'

He thought she had a lovely smile, when she found it.

'Still,' he said. 'Christmas.'

He had always enjoyed Christmas on Earth. It brought out the best in its inhabitants. He began to wonder if he would see another one before his song came to an end, as Ood Sigma had promised it would. Then he shut down the thought and listened to the biodome birdsong again as he followed Adelaide.

At least the birds were still alive in there, he thought. That had to be a good sign.

On the other side of the biodome, Tarak was listening to the birds, too. He often visited the biodome when he was off duty. It puzzled him that more of his crewmates didn't find the same comfort there that he did. It was the closest to being on Earth that any of them were going to get for the next five years. And here there was zero air pollution and zero unwanted noise to break its natural enchantment. He would go there, take a book and let the birdsong and the scent of the place fill his head. Andy had once caught him asleep there among the bushes and had hosed him down with icy water. Andy had sworn that he had been watering the plants and hadn't seen him, but Tarak knew Andy better than that.

And it had just been his bad luck to run into the

captain as he made his way, soaking wet, back to his quarters. She was – as he had told the Doctor – a remarkable woman, but she had barely a playful bone in her body. He often wondered what she had been like as a child; bookish and brooding, he thought. No matter what her achievements might have been in leading Earth's conquest of Mars, it was a wasted childhood – and more – to be so focused on the evasion of fun.

That was when he heard the trickle of water. It sounded a little like a small stream. Tarak knew there weren't any streams in the biodome. But he remembered the soaking that Andy had treated him to. He wondered if there was a hosepipe running.

He followed the sound and came across a small clearing close to the southern side of the dome. Dimly he could see the barren Martian surface beyond its transparent wall.

Before him, Andy stood alone with his back to Tarak, looking out over the desert of dust and rock.

'Hey, Andy.'

At sight of him, Tarak had forgotten about the sound of water that had led him there. His crewmate was standing motionless, with his head bowed, but at least he wasn't unconscious as Maggie had been, and if he had suffered some kind of breakdown – as Ed Gold had suggested – standing motionless didn't suggest any kind of danger. Tarak took a couple of steps towards him. And then he remembered the water.

Andy's arms were held to his sides, and water was trickling from his fingers to the ground.

'Andy?'

Even as Tarak wondered about where the water was coming from, he now realised it wasn't just trickling from Andy's fingers, it was seeping through his sleeves, was running down his back and legs, through his hair, and down his neck. The water was flowing out of Andy's body itself.

Tarak stopped and raised the comms to his mouth. Despite the moist warmth of the biodome, Tarak's hand trembled. 'Captain . . .' he whispered.

Andy spun round. Tarak caught a glimpse of his face. It was no longer the face of his crewmate and friend. The skin was greenish-white, like the face of a drowned corpse, its flesh laced with blackened cracks from which water seeped. The eyes were horrible, clouded orbs.

'Tarak? Tarak, report!'

He barely heard Adelaide's voice coming from his comms unit as the thing before him – the creature that had once been Andy Stone – opened its mutilated mouth. A spray of impossibly icy water shot out of its throat and hit Tarak full in the face.

The Doctor stood beside Adelaide amid the trees and the bushes of the biodome. Suddenly, all this incredible, improbable beauty had turned into a nightmare.

A nightmare he had no business being part of. And yet, here he was.

'Tarak, talk to me!' Adelaide snapped into the comms unit. And again they heard it over the comms: that gargled snarl of inhuman threat.

Next moment, the Doctor was plunging headlong through the foliage, the way Tarak had gone to check on that external door. 'Come on Adelaide! This way! Quick!'

They ran hard, ignoring the pathways, the Doctor relying on an instinctive sense of direction, finding the fastest way through the trees and bushes.

And into the clearing.

The instant he saw them, he spread out an arm to stop Adelaide.

'No closer!' he whispered.

Ahead of them, Tarak was on his knees, his head bowed. Andy stood over him, his hand placed on Tarak's skull. It almost looked like a blessing, an anointing. But Andy's outstretched hand, etched with cracked blackened skin, was flowing with water that cascaded through Tarak's hair and over his shoulders. Andy's mouth was open, and the Doctor could see water spilling from the frayed and blackened lips. Again, they heard its growl.

Tarak's body began to shudder and jerk in a circle of reclaimed Martian soil, as water seeped from crevices in his own cracking flesh.

Horrified Adelaide pulled the pulse pistol that was still clipped to her belt and took a step forward. 'Professor Stone, I'm ordering you to step away from that man!'

The Doctor watched as she took another step towards them. 'Don't get any closer, Adelaide!'

She didn't. That was when Andy turned his head towards them, and they saw the full horror of what he had become. He stared at her with opaque, drowned eyes.

Cautiously, the Doctor drew closer to Adelaide, who was still pointing the gun at Andy Stone's head.

'Andy, can you hear me?' he called, like he was trying to coax a man down from a roof. 'I know you've got bad stuff going on, but believe me, I can help you. Just move away from Tarak, let him go, and listen to me. Please. OK?'

The Doctor had no idea if Andy could hear him or, if he did, if he still had the ability to understand. But, slowly, Andy moved his hand away from Tarak. Water still poured from the raw skin of his palm and fingers to batter the Martian soil below. At the same time Tarak's body stopped its spasms; he just stayed kneeling on the ground, head bowed, motionless.

'That's better, Andy. Hello. We didn't meet earlier. I'm the Doctor.'

That was when the growl came again. This time from Tarak, as he got to his feet and turned towards them. The Doctor took an instinctive step backwards. Tarak looked like a soaking wet cadaver, water seeping from blackened splits in the flesh. He and Andy stood together like corpses just dragged from a pool yet somehow standing shoulder to shoulder, watching the Doctor and Adelaide with hideous fogged eyes, pin-pricked with dead black pupils.

Adelaide trained the gun on both of them. 'Whatever you are, you're not Tarak and Andy.'

The Doctor saw her jaw set with horrified determination and her finger tensed against the trigger. The two soaked men stared at her, motionless, as if daring her to do it. Or as if they knew it would make no difference.

And the Doctor realised that Adelaide couldn't pull the trigger; whatever she might say, they were her crewmen, and their lives were her responsibility. She couldn't kill them.

Gently he took the gun from her, and she didn't resist. She looked at him and for a moment he could see a lost and frightened small girl.

'It's all right, Adelaide,' the Doctor said softly. 'But we have to go. Right now.'

As the drowned figures started to come for them.

Chapter 6

Isolation

Maggie had woken up ten minutes earlier.

She found Yuri smiling at her from the far side of a plate-glass window as he checked her vital signs on the sickbay monitors. 'Welcome back, soldier,' he said. 'How are you feeling?'

Maggie raised herself off the bed in the isolation tank with one arm and immediately felt pain skewer through her head.

'Ow, eh?' said Yuri.

'What am I doing here?' she asked, as the pain eased a little and she looked around.

'We were very much hoping you could tell us that. Don't you remember anything?'

She bowed her head as she tried to put the fragments of her memory back together in some sort of order. 'I was working in the biodome. Taking readings.'

'We found you in the tunnel outside,' Yuri said, his cheery bedside manner slipping. 'It looked to me as if you were running from something.'

She looked at him, puzzled and worried: 'From what?'

Yuri sat on an office chair and wheeled across to the observation window. He could almost have touched her but for the plate glass. 'Was Andy with you?' he asked.

'Yes!' The memory of him came vividly through the fog that seemed to be filling her brain. 'He dug up his first vegetable. A carrot.'

'A carrot?' Yuri grinned. 'The first carrot on Mars! We make history again! Is that the last you remember?' He could see the strain on her face as she tried to make her brain give up what had happened to her in the biodome, like it was a physical labour. 'Maybe you should just lie back and rest for a while,' he suggested. 'You're safe here.'

Maggie looked around the confines of the isolation tank with new concern. 'Why am I in here?'

'Captain's orders.' Yuri softened the news with another big smile. 'Don't worry. You know what a stickler she is for regulations. Any unexplained medical emergency must be followed by twenty-four hours' isolation and observation.'

'But I'm fine. Let me out. Come on, Yuri.'

He wasn't surprised that she was complaining about it. They were already confined enough here on the base. No wonder she didn't like the idea of the isolation tank.

'What is it with you, Maggie? You want to see Captain Adelaide roast me like a hog?' He knew he was in enough trouble already after the stranger broadcast the big news about him and Mia, even if everybody said they had known all along; it was in the public domain now, and he just knew the captain would find a reason to slap him in the face with it sooner or later. 'Take my advice and make the most of the downtime.'

Maggie eased herself back down onto the bed and watched the Russian go back to his monitor screens. She heard him contact Control and tell Ed Gold that she had recovered consciousness and seemed well, considering they had found her in the tunnel with a head trauma. Her fingers found the dressing on her forehead. Yuri said he thought she had been running away from something, but what? The last thing she could remember was Andy brandishing the carrot as she took a photograph. He was going to eat it, he said, right there in the Garden of Eden the two of them had created together. And he had left her to her bio-readings to wash off the Martian dirt under a standpipe.

She was running away.

Surely it couldn't have been from Andy?

He was like her brother. He would never hurt her.

And yet . . .

She watched through the glass as Yuri left his seat and got himself a drink from the water cooler. A big bubble of air appeared in the transparent cylinder as he filled his cup. It quickly reached the surface, absorbed into the level of air that sat above the liquid in the tank.

Water.

She had seen the same reaction a million times in countless water coolers just like this one. It was a simple phenomenon that was all about air pressure. Bowie's air pressure was artificially maintained at 1013.25 millibars, the equivalent to sea-level atmospheric pressure on Earth, so the phenomenon of air replacing water in a cooler was exactly the same. Yet now Maggie felt bizarrely compelled by the process, as if she had never seen it before.

Water, her memory whispered. *There was something about water . . .*

It was a simple inorganic chemical element comprised of one oxygen and two hydrogen atoms. In its pure form it was tasteless, odourless and colourless. It provided neither food, energy, nor organic micronutrients, and yet it was the most basic building block to all life. Human beings were so densely made up of it, it was said that that on Earth the gravitational pull of its moon that created ocean tides could also affect people. An average 160-pound man was made up of sixty pounds of water. Maggie's body was sixty per cent water, and right now she could feel every atom of it circulating through her body; in her blood, in her flesh, in her organs, her lungs and the air she breathed.

And it was whispering to her.

*

Yuri glanced across at Maggie in the isolation tank as he finished drawing water from the cooler; she was lying on the bed with her eyes closed, taking nurse's orders like a good patient.

He returned to his chair and tried to raise Tarak on his comms but got nothing except static. They had expected some pretty harsh solar radiation bursts that could knock out Earth communications; maybe it was screwing up the microwave connections between handhelds on the base, too. He decided not to worry about it. Tarak would be back soon enough to look after his patient in the isolation tank.

He pulled up a personal communications file on the computer. It was a transmission from his brother Mikhail that had come through a week earlier. Like all the Bowie crew, Yuri prized the video calls he got from family on Earth and would watch them repeatedly, the way the history documentaries said their predecessors would read paper-and-ink letters that would have been delivered to their doors by people carrying heavy sacks of similar documents. *And they said his generation had had it hard the last four decades!*

Mikhail came on screen. He was Yuri's younger brother, and he was complaining – as always – about his husband. George was an Englishman that Mikhail had met during a university exchange programme; they had fallen for each other as hard as a couple of lumberjacked redwoods, and George had gone back to

Russia with his brother. Yuri couldn't blame Mikhail; George was a good-looking blond boy with a smile that could light up a city and a dimple in his chin deeper than some Martian craters. But he had the fiscal temperament of a toddler taking a hammer to his piggy bank. Mikhail was always complaining about George's latest extravagance – like the time George had bought him a new car for his birthday and put the whole thing on Mikhail's credit account.

'It's the thought that counts, he says,' Mikhail had grumbled on the video call and then broken into a smile. 'God, I could eat him up like chak-chak!'

'Is that your brother?' he heard Maggie ask from behind him in the isolation tank as he played the video call. Mikhail was talking in Russian. Without looking round, Yuri explained how Mikhail made him laugh, how he was always talking about George like he was a total disaster area but loved him like the sweetest dessert.

'Where does he live?' she asked.

'Just outside Dagestan. Here, I'll show you.'

The screen filled with some touristy pictures of the area.

'They are very lucky. It's beautiful there, right on the Caspian Sea,' he told her.

On one of the photographs, the sea spread out into the horizon, as blue as the sky above it.

'So much water,' she said quietly behind him. 'So much water.'

'Very different to Mars,' he agreed, still scrolling through the pictures of Dagestan and the Caspian beyond it, a part of him thinking about how it would feel one day to jump into those blue waters once more and swim. 'Though, of course, strictly speaking, the Caspian is a lake, not a sea. Over 300,000 square kilometres of water. I don't care, I just want to jump in. Eh, Maggie?'

He wheeled the chair round to look at Maggie, and that was when he saw the water streaming out of her.

Chapter 7

The Flood

The Doctor and Adelaide were trampling through the first vegetation on Mars in more than a million years. The carefully nurtured leaves and stems and flowers and fruit fell broken and crushed as they ploughed headlong through the biodome.

Behind them came the creatures that were once Andy Stone and Tarak Ital. The Doctor threw a quick glance over his shoulder; whatever had taken possession of the crewmen's bodies and triggered this bizarre watery metamorphosis, it hadn't slowed them down. The two creatures ran fast and determined, shrieking as they came; a kind of viscid war cry, filled with rheum and bile.

The screams were getting closer.

Adelaide's foot caught on a root, and she went down heavily. The Doctor stopped, spun round, grabbed her and pulled her into thick bushes before the creatures caught up. Scrabbling through the branches, he and Adelaide pulled as deeply as they could into the foliage and lay still together on the reddish Martian soil, holding their breath. Through the branches and leaves the Doctor saw their possessed pursuers come to a stop and look around, trying to work out which way their quarry had fled.

He took the opportunity to study the creatures as best he could. How they exuded water was fascinating. It was as if their bodies were covered in a constantly flowing second liquid skin. Although he could see wet footprints in the dirt behind them, they weren't drenching the ground where they now paused, there was no growing pool of water. Somehow their bodies were reabsorbing the water as it spilled over them. The running water wasn't a product of their bodies like perspiration, it was an element of its function, in the same way that he and Adelaide drew breath. Water was a constituent part of human beings; with these creatures it was their structure. Andy and Tarak's bodies simply gave it shape.

There were low growls, the rasping gurgle of waterlogged lungs and throats, as the two of them considered which way to take their hunt. The Doctor couldn't hear a language in the sounds, but he was convinced it was communication. Yet were these creatures intelligent or simply driven by an apparent drive to convert others into their kind, as Andy had with Tarak?

As the Doctor and Adelaide watched, the creatures moved off together into the biodome and were soon obscured by the vegetation.

'What's happened to them, Doctor?' Adelaide demanded in a hushed voice, creeping back out from the bushes.

'I don't know.' The Doctor followed her. 'I think they've been infected.'

'By what, for God's sake?'

'Some sort of microbial life form. In the water.'

Adelaide paled. '*Our* water?'

She reached for her comms unit. It wasn't there. Somewhere during their breakneck run through the trees and bushes the device must have been torn from her belt.

'I have to warn the rest of the crew,' she said. There was no panic in her voice, just determined pragmatism. 'They mustn't touch the water.'

'No,' the Doctor agreed. 'Not one drop.'

Cautiously, they moved off. They reached the airlock quickly, seeing no more sign of Andy or Tarak.

Until they were at the airlock door. Then both water creatures came out of the foliage behind them.

But the creatures didn't come after them. They just stood there, eyes white and unblinking, silent. The silence was worse somehow than the hideous water-logged growl.

'Adelaide,' the Doctor hissed, 'get that airlock door open now!'

Adelaide quickly punched in the passcode as the creatures both raised their right arms, palms pointing towards her, dripping. The Doctor heard the heavy clunk of the airlock bolts disengaging and hauled the door open. He and Adelaide ducked through – as the creatures fired huge jets of water from open palms.

The water hit the heavy door with the force of a crashing wave as the Doctor slammed it shut, leaving him and Adelaide secure inside the airlock.

'Maximum seals,' he ordered, and Adelaide's fingers moved fast over the control panel.

'Engaged,' she answered.

Together they looked through the thick glass of the airlock window. Tarak and Andy were drawing closer.

Well, that settled the question about their intelligence, the Doctor thought. 'They ambushed us,' he said. 'Anticipated our moves. Worked to a plan.'

Adelaide turned to the comms on the airlock wall: 'Attention all crew, this is Captain Brooke. Nobody touch the water. Our water supply has been compromised. Close off all pipes immediately, that's an order.'

Ed came back over the speaker. He was calm, but it didn't hide the tension in his voice. 'Confirmed, Captain. But we've got other problems. Maggie – she's undergone some kind of transformation.'

Adelaide flashed a glance at the Doctor who was still at the window. The creatures that had been Andy and Tarak were both right outside the door now looking in with those blank white eyes.

'Anything?' the Doctor was saying, mostly to himself as he studied them close-up. He tapped experimentally on the glass, like they were fish in a tank. 'Can you speak?'

'Keep her confined in isolation and watch her until I get back. Brooke out.' Adelaide joined the Doctor at the window where the two creatures were laying their hands on the frame of the heavy airlock door, as if ready to wrench it from its huge steel hinges. Instead, water began to surge over it, obscuring the view through the window with heavy cascading curtains.

'They can't get in,' said Adelaide. 'This is airtight and therefore watertight.'

But the Doctor was grim. 'Depends how smart the water is.'

Behind Adelaide, electronics on the airlock wall started to spark and bang.

'They're fusing the system!'

'Abandon ship!' the Doctor cried. He was already opening the door into the connecting tunnel.

Adelaide followed him out and pushed the door shut. Small but deadly explosions were still going off inside the airlock as its operating systems were destroyed by the water that now sprayed around the edges of the biodome door. As she looked, the door opened inwards and the Andy and Tarak creatures stepped into the empty airlock.

'Doctor, we have to get out of here fast,' Adelaide

gasped. 'With the airlock's systems compromised, this might as well be a saloon door in a cowboy movie.'

The Doctor saw Andy's drowned and mutilated face already at the airlock door window. He looked around. They had left Gadget on patrol and the odd-looking robot was now about a hundred metres away.

'Gadget!' he yelled and was racing towards it with Adelaide close behind.

As they reached it, the airlock door swung open with a gush of water that spilled over its step and swirled across the tunnel floor.

'Jump on board!' the Doctor instructed, pulling out the sonic screwdriver.

Adelaide shook her head. 'Gadget only moves at two miles an hour!'

Behind them, the terrifying creatures were sweeping towards them. Water had no moving parts to slow it down, it was one ultra-simple body of super-viscosity – even as the things that had once been Andy and Tarak ran like men, they moved with the speed of rushing water.

The Doctor ran the sonic screwdriver over Gadget's control processors and jumped onto the small cargo deck behind its head. 'Two miles an hour? You'd better buckle up.' As Adelaide jumped on board behind him, he used the sonic screwdriver again and the robot squawked in something that sounded like surprise.

'*Gadget-Gadget*!'

And suddenly they were hurtling down the tunnel like they were astride a fast motorbike, not riding a homemade robot with caterpillar tracks. The Doctor risked a look back over his shoulder. He saw the water men were still coming, running with a bizarre, impossibly fast liquid grace. But Gadget was leaving them behind. The air was filled with the smell of burning rubber. Gadget's caterpillars, never intended for anything like this furious speed, were combusting as the robot roared through the tunnel, leaving fiery tracks behind.

'*Gaaaaaaaaaaaaaadget!*'

Although Adelaide couldn't see the Doctor's face – he had his back to her as he held Gadget's shoulders like a couple of oversized handlebars – she suspected he might be smiling. Not for the first time in the last hour or so, she wanted to know just who this man was, where he came from, how he knew what he knew – and just exactly what it was that he did know.

They had left the Andy and Tarak creatures a long way back in the tunnel by the time they reached the airlock to the Central Dome. But Adelaide knew they would catch up soon enough. She jumped down and got the airlock open.

'The Central Dome airlocks all have Hardinger seals,' she said. 'They got through the biodome airlock, but they can't get through a door like this.' She turned to see the Doctor urgently ushering Gadget up the ramp to the open airlock; if a robot could ever look exhausted, she thought, that was Gadget. 'I thought you hated robots?'

'I do,' he said.

But somehow Adelaide felt there were very few things that the Doctor would truly hate.

They got the airlock door shut seconds before the water creatures caught up to them. Once again, those strange, corrupted eyes were staring in at them.

'They can't get in,' she told him again, and wondered for an instant if she was really just trying to convince herself.

'Water is patient, Adelaide,' the Doctor told her. 'Water just waits. It wears down mountains, it eats away clifftops, it shapes whole worlds. Water always wins.'

With a last look at the water creatures held at the gates – at least for now – the Doctor opened the door into the Central Dome. Together they made their way to the medical facility.

They found Ed there with Yuri, both transfixed by the metamorphosised Maggie, who stood with her palms pressed against the toughened glass of the isolation tank. Water spilled from her hands, from between her cracked lips, over her whole body. It almost looked like she was smiling as she watched them watching her.

'Adelaide, thank God you're back,' Ed said.

Quickly she brought the two men up to speed on what had happened in the biodome, and what had become of their two other crewmates.

Yuri looked scared. 'Are you sure it's something in the water? We can't drink it?'

'We can't be sure of anything,' said Adelaide. 'It's a precaution.'

The Doctor was pressed up to the glass on their side, examining every feature of Maggie's painfully deformed face. On her side of the glass, Maggie's strange eyes seemed to be doing the same to him.

'Can she talk?' Adelaide asked.

'I don't know,' Yuri answered. 'She was talking before she changed. She seemed very interested in the Caspian Sea.'

That made the Doctor look across at him.

Adelaide had drawn closer to the glass. 'Maggie, can you hear me? Maggie Caine, this is Captain Adelaide Brooke. If you can understand me, make some kind of signal. I need to know what happened to you.'

The Maggie water creature had turned its gaze to the Bowie Base commander at the sound of her voice, but made no sign of understanding, as far as the Doctor could see.

He said: '*Hoorghwall in schtochman ahn warrellinsh och fortabellan iin hoorgwahn.*'

Adelaide and the others stared at him.

'What the hell was that?' Ed demanded.

'Ancient Martian. *North* Martian, to be precise,' the Doctor answered, not taking his eyes off Maggie.

Adelaide rolled her eyes. 'Don't be ridiculous.'

'What? Every planet has a North,' said the Doctor.

'I saw a flicker in her eyes,' Yuri told them uncertainly. 'Like maybe she recognised it.'

'North Martian,' Adelaide repeated, not sure what to believe any more.

'Where does your water come from?'

'The ice field,' Ed told him. 'It's why the surveyors put us here. We're on top of a subterranean glacier.'

'Tons and tons of ice,' the Doctor observed grimly. 'Marvellous.'

'But it's all filtered and screened,' Yuri argued. 'It's safe.'

The Doctor nodded, his eyes going back to the creature in the isolation tank. 'Looks like it, yeah.'

Adelaide was thinking through what they had seen in the biodome and now here. 'You're saying that if something was frozen down there, some kind of viral life form, for all these millennia, it would have been perfectly preserved, just waiting for a host to come along?'

'And humans are sixty per cent water,' the Doctor observed. 'The *perfect* hosts. But look at Maggie. The water never stops, it pours out of her mouth and exudes from her skin. This thing, whatever it is, doesn't just hide in water. It *creates* water.'

'Is that really possible?' Adelaide asked.

The Doctor said nothing, just gestured to Maggie Cain standing in the observation tank.

And in a drowned aqueous voice, words spilled out of what had been Maggie's mouth: 'The Flood shall rise. And the waters will take you all.'

'The Flood?' The Doctor bobbed closer to the glass, energised by the water creature's proclamation. 'Is that you? Is that your consciousness?'

'We have waited. So long. For the return of the Flesh.'

'Is she talking about us? The Flesh?' Yuri sounded disgusted.

'You have so much water,' Maggie said in that cold, inhuman voice. 'You will drown in the Flood. Everyone drowns. And we will be free.'

'Free?' the Doctor demanded. 'To do what? What is it you want?'

Her eyes raised over his head. There was a clock on the wall like the one he had seen in the Bowie control room, showing Mars, a red desert planet, and Earth with its white clouds of water vapor and vast blue seas.

'So much water,' said the drowned voice.

And Adelaide knew.

The Flood wanted Earth.

Chapter 8

Action One

Ed ushered Adelaide into what had been Tarak's office off the sickbay ward. She noticed that one drawer of his desk was open. He had drawn it out and would now never close it. There was a beautiful, intricately decorated prayer mat in a corner of the room on which he would never again kneel. She felt a sudden wave of sorrow and tragedy.

The Australian wasn't giving himself time for reflection or loss. 'This is an unknown infection, and it's spreading,' he said, urgent and business-like. 'It demands Action Procedure One.'

Adelaide glared at him. 'Do you think I don't know that?'

He drew his voice down. 'I think you need reminding.'

She nodded. 'Yeah.'

He smiled. 'At least I'm good for something.'

She returned his smile. 'Now and again.'

Ed raised an eyebrow. 'That's almost a compliment. Things must be serious.'

Adelaide touched his arm. It was the briefest sign of affection, but she saw in Ed's face that he felt it keenly.

She hadn't noticed the Doctor leaning in the doorway, and she and Ed sprang apart like guilty teens as he interrupted: 'Sorry, but Action One, that means evacuation, doesn't it? Evacuation of the base.'

'Yes. We're abandoning Bowie Base One.' Even as she spoke the words, she couldn't believe she was saying them. It was something she had never imagined. Even as, back on Earth, they had rehearsed every kind of disaster scenario, Adelaide had never once seriously considered the idea of giving up.

She took Ed's comms unit from his belt and spoke: 'Attention Bowie Base One. This is Captain Brooke. I am initiating Action Procedure One. I repeat, Action One. Begin evacuation procedures.' She closed her eyes for a moment, coming to terms with what she had to do. 'We're going home.'

In the control room, Steffi reacted just the way Adelaide knew she would, with urgent calm competence, ordering Mia to strip the cargo down to essentials while she detached and stored away Bowie's central computer core. The two women worked like they had trained for it.

But Roman sat disbelievingly at his console with Gadget. 'We came all this way . . .'

'The mission is terminated, Roman,' Steffi said simply. 'And you can kiss your robot goodbye, it's too heavy for an emergency launch. Put it in storage. Now move!'

She watched as Roman slouched out of his chair. She knew he couldn't believe any of this was happening any more than she could. After all the training, the years of prep before that. They had come to Mars as heroes, doing what no one had ever been able to do before them, and being recognised all around the world for it. Now they were fleeing, scared. And why? Because of water.

Adelaide was still on the comms. She was asking Steffi how long it would take to get the shuttle launch-ready.

'It's a seven month flight, Captain,' Steffi responded. 'It will take a minimum of three hours to get everything aboard that we need.'

Adelaide came back: 'You've got an hour!'

Steffi stiffened, but kept her voice steady: 'Yes, Captain.'

'And give me a report on Andy and Tarak.'

Steffi brought up a camera on one of the monitor screens: it gave her a high-angle shot of the two hid eous creatures that had once been her crewmates for seventeen months on Mars. 'They're just standing in the tunnel looking at the camera.'

'Keep an eye on them,' Adelaide told her.

Like I don't have enough work to do? 'Aye-aye, Captain.'

Roman looked at Gadget. There had never been any mission requirement for a drone or a robot. Gadget was nothing more than scavenged tech that he had put together in his downtime during the first couple of months on Mars. But the bot had quickly proved its worth.

It wasn't just his greatest contribution to Bowie Base One, Roman thought. It was the best thing he had done in his life. He'd sometimes imagined Gadget as the prototype of a whole new range of space pioneering robots that would make their way across the solar system and beyond, in preparation for the humans that would follow. Or if that seemed unlikely, how about his own line of action figures, entrancing a generation of space-struck kids? Corporatisation of space was the big thing, now, and getting bigger with every mission. He had imagined the TV ads for it – a Gadget could be every kid's robot friend. Not a bad side-hustle, he had thought.

But now he was going to have to pack Gadget in a crate and leave the robot discarded in the Bowie stores, and make-believe that someone might come back for it someday. More likely, once they got back to Earth, Gadget would be forgotten. By everyone but Roman.

His eyes were wet when he closed the crate on his spare-part friend.

Meanwhile, the Doctor was still leaning in the doorway of Tarak's office. Behind him Yuri had started boxing up medical supplies, yanking open drawers and cabinets and throwing meds and dressings and kit into containers. The Doctor had no doubt that when Adelaide Brooke gave an order, people got busy. She was sending Ed back to Control. He was the shuttle's pilot and she wanted it prepped for launch in twenty minutes – the water creatures were all locked up or locked out for now, but if that changed she wanted to be able to launch immediately. Ed was on it and brushed quickly past the Doctor on his way out.

Adelaide had kept hold of Ed's comms unit. She clipped it to her belt and looked at the Doctor. 'Your spacesuit will be returned. You're free to leave any time you want. And the best of luck to you.'

'Thanks. But the only problem with evacuation, Adelaide, is that this thing is clever. The Flood didn't infect the birds in the biodome – they are flesh creatures, too, remember, made up of water – it chose the humans.'

Adelaide pushed past him, back into the sickbay ward. 'The Flood wants to get to Earth, Doctor. Not much chance of that if they took over the sparrows.'

He followed her. 'I just told you, the problem is, it's clever.'

'And I've told you I have a base to evacuate.' She headed for the door.

The Doctor stepped in front of it. 'Adelaide, water can wait!'

'Which means what, exactly?'

'Tarak changed straight away. Andy too, probably. But when Maggie was infected the Flood stayed hidden inside her – probably so that it could infiltrate the Central Dome. It *waited*.'

Adelaide froze as the implication hit her. 'You mean any of us could be a host? We've all been drinking the same water. Anyone could be infected.'

The Doctor nodded slowly. 'If you take that back to Earth, Adelaide. One drop. Just one drop . . . All Earth could be infected.'

Adelaide paced away from him and back again, as if measuring the chance that he was right. 'All right. We can't risk carrying this thing back to Earth. But the only way this infection could have started is if there was a fault in the filtration process of our water from the glacier. If we can pinpoint when that happened, it might show us that no one's drawn fresh water since then. Maybe we've still got a chance.'

The Doctor forced a hopeful smile. 'Maybe.' He stood aside for her, and she went through the door. 'Where are you going?' he asked.

'The ice field.'

He watched her head down the corridor. Adelaide Brooke, as determined as ever. Determined to do whatever it took to save her crew. The things they would write about her courage and commitment were all true. But it would all be for nothing; she couldn't save them. And nor could he.

'Right,' he said to himself. 'I should leave. Finally, I should leave.' He looked back into the sickbay. Yuri was still working furiously to pack up the medical supplies. Beyond him he could see the Maggie creature behind the observation window; water still spilled from her mouth, disfigured lips still in some kind of obscene smile; her dead eyes watching Yuri as he prepared for the evacuation that the Doctor knew would never happen.

I really, really should leave.

There was no point in him seeing the ice field, was there?

No point at all!

As he chased after Adelaide.

Chapter 9

The Woman with Starlight in Her Soul

There had been a camp the night before the Earth was stolen. Adelaide had lain on the ground outside her tent with Julie Price and Adya Dutta, head-to-head in a three-girl wheel looking up at the stars.

It was a warm Friday night and quiet but for the camp chatter of the other girls on the site. It was the first camp for each spoke of the wheel as Girl Guides; they had all turned ten that year, and it was the first time they would be away from their parents for almost a full week.

They were practically adults now, Julie had said proudly, thrilling at the prospect of five days away from home during half term. Adelaide had embraced the same expectation with a combination of relief and dread: her parents had spent most of the last six months fighting. Mostly they did it in secret, of course, and camouflaged whatever was wrong between them behind smiles and difficult silences, but she was their only child and she was ten now: she knew when people were fighting, no matter how quietly they went about it. So Adelaide was relieved to escape the atmosphere in the house but, at the same time, what she might find on her return scared her.

All the same, she was determined to try and enjoy her first Guide camp and the company of her two best friends. Whether or not they were 'practically adults' now, Adelaide had a sense that there was change coming. Maybe it was the emerging fractures in her parents' relationship, or the knowledge of the changes that would soon start in her own body, but the comfort she had felt all her life, the assurances both spoken and inferred that everything was – and always would be – all right, was slipping away.

She had known Julie and Adya since their first day at infant school, they had been friends forever, they were a constant that she would hang on to no matter how the world transformed around them. So, together, they lay on the grass and contemplated the heavens and talked about school, boys and Lady Gaga, and Adya wondered if somewhere up above them there might be three girls lying on the grass of another world looking back.

There were sometimes stories about aliens coming to Earth in the newspapers; they had all seen so-called witness testimony online. But Adelaide told them that if spacemen had really been visiting their planet for centuries, like some people claimed, how come all they had were stories? How come there was no evidence?

Julie countered that the evidence existed, but the governments hid it with the help of their military. That's what UNIT was for, she told them assuredly. She had read it online. They had a secret place called the Black Archive where they kept all kinds of extraterrestrial stuff. They had all the evidence Adelaide could want.

Adelaide had heard of UNIT; every now and again they would show up in the background of a TV news story, running about in their red berets. 'But if this Black Archive is so secret, how come you can read about it on the net?' she wanted to know.

'Whistle-blowers,' Adya told her.

Adelaide had seen the term online. Teachers blew whistles to get them back into class after break, calling time on their fun. She guessed the term sort of fitted when it came to someone calling the government out on their secrets of alien visitation. But this was the military they were talking about. Did her friends really think if the army had this big secret about spacemen coming to Earth, and they had alien technology and God-knew what squirrelled away some place, would they really let someone get away with putting it on the internet? No, they'd lock them up, or shoot them.

'Or wipe their memories,' Julie said enthusiastically, not grasping what little good it did her whole argument.

'Yeah,' Adelaide said. 'Or that.'

And that was pretty much their holding position on the matter when they turned in for the night, zipped up their tent and got into their sleeping bags. Tomorrow would be Saturday; they'd got archery in the morning and canoeing in the afternoon. Breakfast was in the big community tent at eight.

The three of them fell asleep quickly and woke up to the rallying call over the camp's speakers at seven-fifteen. The scent of the pine trees that bordered the scout camp was in the air and the sky was bright blue with only a few slowly passing white clouds. They got ready and were heading into the community tent with the rest of the troop by eight. They were in the queue for their meals when the ground started to shake.

'What's that?' Julie asked. Even the baked beans that had just been spooned onto her plate were moving.

'Earthquake,' Adya answered.

'Don't be silly,' Adelaide said. 'They don't have earthquakes in Surrey.'

As the piles of plates on the long servery table started to chatter, the girls and Guide leaders looked around them with accelerating concern.

Then the plates were shattering on the ground, and the tables that filled the community tent were moving, and the canvas walls started to billow furiously as the lines and poles that held the tent up shook in the ground. Suddenly there was screaming everywhere. The servery table collapsed, and its steel trays fell, spraying food across the ground. Somewhere in the panicked cacophony there was the voice of a Guide leader telling everyone to stay calm.

Adelaide grabbed Julie and Adya, and they held each other tight as the earth shook and somehow seemed to lend its own tortured voice from underground to the screaming. Then Adelaide was aware of the tent darkening around them. Her first thought was that they had been gripped by some kind of massive storm; a storm so strong that it could shake the ground under their feet. But the day had been such a beautiful one less than five minutes ago; none of the clouds in the sky as they had crossed the grass to the community tent had been storm clouds. Her eyes turned to the tent doorway which still shook with whatever kind of maelstrom now possessed it, and the darkness beyond it was utterly complete. Darker than any storm she had ever seen, deeper than any night.

And the three of them were thrown to the ground.

It felt as if the entire world had suddenly spasmed – and then, stopped. The shaking had ended. Around Adelaide the screaming and now sobbing continued. People were shaking so much themselves that they hadn't realised the ground had fallen still.

Adelaide got to her feet and began walking through the smashed crockery and spilled food and terrified children towards the tent entrance. Everything was darkness around her. Part of her was wondering why she wasn't shivering and sobbing with fear like so many of the other kids she saw on the ground clinging to the legs of chairs or tables, or each other. She was nervous, yes. She trembled. But it was with curiosity and with anticipation, not fear. Whatever had just happened here she knew that it was far from natural, and more than anything she wanted to understand it.

Then she stood in the tent doorway and looked up and she was a long, long way from understanding. She was closer to being frightened, it was true. And, for the first few moments that she took it all in, her head spun and her chest struggled to pull in air, but that passed as quickly as it had come. But the wonder that she felt would never pass.

Above her was an alien sky of darkness and strange distant stars and other planets that seemed so large and close she could almost reach out with her ten-year-old's hand and touch them.

Adelaide had broken into a jog as she made her way along the tunnel to the ice field. The Doctor came running up behind her soon after.

'How come whoever was clever enough to name this place after a music god, never thought about putting bikes on the cargo manifest?' he wanted to know.

'I like to run,' she told him.

'Or scooters? Scooters are fun.'

'I turned sixty a couple of months ago.'

'Happy birthday.'

'It's not easy being the oldest person on a planet.'

'Yeah,' he said. 'Well, I wouldn't worry too much about that now.'

They reached the door to the ice field. It was a pressure door, but not an airlock, and as Adelaide opened it he felt the slightest breath of colder air on his face. They stepped through and there was a long flight of metal steps going down. Adelaide took them with the agility of a child. Despite her by-the-book veneer, the Doctor was sure there was a part of her that had never grown up. He followed her down the steps, feeling it get colder all the way.

This place wasn't like any other part of Bowie; the steps and the steel platform below it were surrounded by bare rock carved by laser drills mounted on the construction drones that had built it. Attached to the rock was a network of pipes. Pipes that had carried the Flood into the base.

Below them, as the Doctor hurried down the steps behind Adelaide, he saw the ice field. It was a huge bluish-white expanse of ice that filled the natural cavern below them. Its visible surface was breathtaking in its size and there was no telling how deep it went, what its full mass might be. It had been there for millions of years. Countless millennia. Untouched and unseen. Until a survey probe had discovered it and mission-planners on Earth had begun to draw their plans for humanity's first permanent base on Mars.

Water was so very, very patient.

Adelaide reached the platform and crossed to a bank of computers and monitoring equipment. 'We need to find any interruption in the water-processing procedure,' she said. 'Anything abnormal. We have to put a date on the infection.'

The Doctor heard her, but he had paused on the steps, feeling drawn to the gigantic glacier that spread out below. He felt touched by its history. On Earth, scientists had learned so much by drilling deep into the ice packs at the planet's poles. The cores drawn from the polar ice described their own stories about Earth's evolution as a living world. These frozen waters of Mars had their own story, one that was still playing out.

'There are legends of Mars,' he said, more to himself than to Adelaide. 'Of a fine and noble Martian race who built an empire out of ice . . .'

He felt Adelaide looking up at him; she was still by the monitors, and he caught an odd searching look on her face.

'We're running out of time, Doctor,' she said simply. 'We need to be sure that it's safe to return to Earth.'

'Yes. Yes, of course,' he said, leaping gracefully over the guard rail and onto the platform below. Almost in the same movement he pulled spectacles from one of his pockets, slipped them on, and started to scan information rolling over one of the water-processors' monitor screens.

Adelaide turned to work at another station, but this strange man that had shown up unannounced on the Martian surface was worrying her. And God knew she had enough to worry about. It wasn't because she thought he posed any kind of threat – that suspicion had been defused long ago – but . . . but he seemed to have knowledge of so many things that he really couldn't possibly . . .

She found her eyes moving towards him as she

worked at the processing station. He didn't look like a coward, and he didn't act like one – events in the bio-dome confirmed that – but ever since Gadget had brought him into the base, since things had started going wrong, he'd been talking about how important it was that he should leave.

His eyes were fixed on the screen before him. If he was aware of her watching him, he showed no sign.

'You know so much about us,' she said.

'Yeah, well, you're famous.'

'No. It's like you know more. More than you *could* know.'

She caught his eyes flash towards her over the top of those spectacles, 'What does that mean?'

'I don't know,' she said. But she was disturbed, and it went far beyond the horrors she had seen today.

Maybe he sensed that. Maybe he sensed *something*. The way she had once sensed that things were changing, were about to change for ever . . .

He looked across at her from the monitor screen. He spoke quietly, gently, the way she knew parents sometimes spoke when they had difficult things to tell, 'This moment, this precise moment in time . . . I mean, it's only a theory, what do I know? . . . But I think certain moments in time are fixed. Tiny precious moments. But they are so important.'

Whether it was just a theory or not, she could hear the passion in his voice, she could see it in his eyes.

'Everything else is in flux. Anything can happen. But those certain moments, they have to stand.'

And she thought she knew what he meant. She understood; she had lived moments like that.

'This base on Mars, with you, Adelaide Brooke, this is one of those vital moments. Vital to all of history, to all of time. What happens here must always happen.'

She was staring into his eyes, lost in them; lost in all that she knew – somehow – that they had seen; everything that he must know.

'*What happens here must always happen*?' she echoed. 'What is that?'

'. . . I don't know,' he said.

And she was scared.

What she saw in the Doctor's eyes scared her. Because she knew that he was lying.

Perhaps he saw that she knew. He went on: 'I think something wonderful happens. Something that started fifty years ago.'

But he couldn't know that.

'Isn't that right?' he said. 'When you were ten years old.'

'I've never told anyone that.'

But that wasn't entirely true.

'You told your daughter. You told Emily. And maybe one day she tells the story to her daughter.'

Suzie. He mentioned Suzie when he showed up here.

'The day the Earth was stolen and moved across the universe. And you—'

Adelaide broke in: 'I saw the Daleks.'

The confusion and fear inside the Guides' big tent had been nothing compared to what followed when people saw the sky. The scouting motto was to Be Prepared, for anything. But what could prepare anyone for something like this?

'Mind-bender,' Julie gasped with awe when Adelaide got her two friends outside.

Adya started to cry quietly, and Adelaide put her arm around her shoulders. But she didn't even try to say that everything was going to be all right. Quite apart from whatever had happened over their heads it was evident that things on the ground were looking a long way off orderly. Although there were some leaders trying to comfort and reassure the girls, there were other adults on their knees, holding their heads in their hands hopelessly, or praying.

'Is it the end of the world?' Adya asked, her voice hitching with tears.

'No way,' Julie whispered. 'The world's still here – it's just . . . moved.'

'But how can that happen? It's not possible!'

'It doesn't matter how it's happened,' Adelaide insisted. 'We just have to make sure we don't lose our heads over it.'

She saw Adya sniff back tearful snot and nod, reassured by the company of her friends, however this turned out.

'So, what do we do?' Julie said.

Adelaide took in the scene around them. No one was handling this gearshift in reality with anything like fortitude. 'Well,' she said, 'I'm not staying here. If anything else is coming, I want to be under something more than canvas.'

Julie agreed. And Adya wanted her mum and dad. To be honest, so did Adelaide.

They had been driven to the campsite in a coach, but it had left after dropping them off, to return again in five days. There were a couple of cars parked around the site and Julie suggested they find someone to drive one. Adelaide approached some of the adults, but they just told her to sit with the others; the truth was that she didn't trust any of them in their confused state.

So, Adelaide went into the camp office and found a map. They were about thirty miles from home. That was walkable she reckoned. And with luck they might get a lift part way, there were bound to be police cars on patrol, trying to keep order; she bet the army would be on the roads, too. Maybe even Julie's UNIT. Getting a lift in an army truck was going to be a heck of a lot safer than trusting one of the Guide leaders *to get them back into* London, *she thought.*

There were a couple of high-powered torches in the office. Adelaide took them along with the map. Be Prepared, *she thought. She didn't consider it stealing. This was survival.*

Nobody else seemed to notice or try to stop the girls as they packed gear into their backpacks and headed off the campsite. They were all too busy staring at the sky, comforting each other or praying. Adelaide noticed that a couple of the Guide leaders had by now developed their own small congregations of kids in prayer. Her parents weren't especially religious and so neither was she. She doubted that most of the kids she saw on their knees now with their hands pressed together were, either. But Adelaide still had more faith in herself than any kind of universal caretaker in that strange sky that now covered them all.

Together with Julie and Adya – who had stopped crying now they had a plan – Adelaide walked into the woods that surrounded the camp.

None of them had ever been in a forest at night before, and even if the tree canopy meant they couldn't see much of the strange new worlds that hung above them now, it was still a disconcerting, alien place. Each rustle of grass and crack of twig was somehow amplified by the darkness. Adelaide tried to remind herself that it was really just a little after nine in the morning, but it didn't do much good. And, as far as the animals were concerned, it was night-time, and they were letting loose all the cries and screams they usually would after dark.

Briefly Adelaide wondered about the sun – if the Earth wasn't circling it any more (as those strange planets above suggested) – how long before everything started to get cold? Really cold?

One thing at a time, she told herself. There was already enough to worry about, without freaking out over stuff that hadn't happened yet.

Eventually they emerged from the woods, found themselves on a bank and carefully descended until, with relief, they came to a minor road. Adelaide identified it on the map, and they started walking west. They walked for a long time with no sign of a car. Over them hung the black sky and the planets that shouldn't have been there. Out here on the road the world was silent but for the sound of their boots on the tarmac. Alone in the darkness it started to feel like the world really might have ended and all that was left of the human race was three ten-year-old Girl Guides.

They had been walking for a couple of hours, and had seen nobody, when they became aware of new lights in the sky. Not still, like the planets or the unknown stars. These were moving and the girls instinctively hid as they realised what they were. Spaceships. And if evidence had been required – as they had discussed during their hike – that what had happened was of alien origin, it seemed to all three of them that it was on its way.

Maybe they would be safer out in the country, after all. If this was an alien invasion, the ships would be headed for London, along with the other major cities of the world. But London was where their parents would be. That was who they wanted to be with. The lights in the sky became spinning discs, just like people had always claimed they had seen in the papers and those television shows. And, yes, they were headed in the direction of the capital.

The girls came to a main road and there was a sign for London. As they looked, it was lit up by coming headlights.

They heard the approach of a big vehicle and Adelaide hoped it was the army trucks she had half promised herself would come. They were caught in its lights, and it rolled to a stop, its engine still running.

'What the hell are you three doing out here?' they heard a man yell from the cab with an accent.

It wasn't the army. It was an articulated truck full of flowers, not guns. THE TULIP EXPRESS. *Adelaide saw it written on the cab door as the driver opened it and told then to hurry up and get in.*

The girls all knew the rules on strangers, but decided that today the regular conventions no longer applied. Anyway, there were three of them.

The driver was a brawny Dutchman with a black and silver beard that reached his chest. He was called Peter and, as he got the truck moving again, he told them he had come off the ferry at Dover that morning loaded with tulips and daffodils before everything went dark. He said he didn't care what had happened in the sky, he had a truckload of flowers that he was being paid to deliver to florists in London. He was already late, but he was damned if he was going to give anyone an excuse not to pay him. A contract was a contract whether the sky held or fell.

'Flowers are good for the soul,' he told them as they headed for the city. 'From what I see, people could do with some daffodils in their lives right now.'

Adelaide suspected that flowers would the last thing on people's minds, and guessed he was just trying to comfort three ten-year-olds with something that sounded like regular chit-chat as the truck headlights cut through the darkness ahead of them, and they travelled through a world that no longer made sense.

The cab itself had a pungent floral scent, though Adelaide couldn't place it. It seemed to cling to Peter himself, as well. He told them he'd not been able to get anything other than static over his radio and CB since the skies had changed. So, he sang to himself. Adelaide tried to work out if it was the kind of thing he would do anyway, or if it was again his way of reassuring them. Whichever, his singing ran out as they travelled through the urban areas that bordered London. It was a disaster zone.

There were broken windows, people looting from shops, they saw a couple of police cars on fire, some fights. They passed houses where people had barricaded themselves in. A supermarket was burning, and they heard no fire sirens signalling anyone was coming to put it out. Peter steered the flower truck through the chaos, and no one spoke. The girls wondered what they would find when they reached home.

They had started to see other vehicles now, mostly on the other side of the road as people tried to escape the city. But they also started to see military vehicles loaded with soldiers. Peter told them it was a good sign – the soldiers would help keep order. Soon after that they got their first proper sighting of one of the spaceships. The shock of it made Peter hit the brakes sharply and they all lurched in the cab.

It was stationary over the city, a huge slowly rotating

saucer with lights on its underside that glowed with shifting colours. It was, Adelaide thought, both a terrifying and wonderful thing. Something she had never really dreamed of seeing detached from a movie screen. A part of her – of all of them – still told her that it, and everything else they were seeing, wasn't actually real. It was all one very weird dream from which soon they would all wake, and Adelaide and her friends would find archery classes and canoeing club waiting for them.

But as they moved on, the roads became quiet and deserted again, and in the distance they began to hear the sound of gunfire. Short, repeated bursts of automatic rifles. And other sounds that they didn't understand, buzzes that sounded like pulses of energy, and strange electronic voices barking commands that they couldn't make out.

And screaming.

Adelaide saw Adya and Julie looking at her in the darkness of the cab. Their eyes were wide with fear. She didn't think her own eyes would look any different to them.

As they rolled toward Chiswick High Road, they saw a column of people, their hands on their heads, being herded along a road by what Adelaide at first thought looked like big metal bins with stalks protruding from them. Peter immediately stopped the truck again and turned off his lights.

'What in God's name are those?' he breathed, leaning forward over the wheel.

As they watched, a second group of people were herded

into the street by the metallic beings, and Adelaide could hear those strange voices clearly now.

'We are the Daleks! You will obey!'

'Obey or be exterminated!'

Daleks, thought Adelaide. These things were what had come from the spaceships, and they weren't here to make friends.

'I'm sorry, girls. I think this is as close to home as I can get you. You should get out now.' Peter told them quietly. His voice was different now, she thought, there was no reassurance in it. His eyes were fixed on the Daleks ahead and their human captives.

Adelaide calculated that the truck was only a few streets away from their homes. They were small, and if they stuck to the shadows maybe they could avoid any more of the Daleks.

'What are you going to do?' she asked Peter.

'Deliver my daffodils,' he told her. 'Be careful, kids. I hope you find your parents OK. Stay safe.'

In the darkness, the girls climbed down from the cab and moved quickly into the cover of shadow. Behind them they heard the flower truck's engine come to life again. Peter turned his lights on high beam and pulled on the truck's horn as it lurched forward at speed.

Along the High Road, Adelaide saw the Daleks swing around, lit up brightly by the oncoming flower truck. Their captives ran for it. Peter was delivering his flowers, but not to any florist shop.

She saw bursts of energy spit from the Daleks' weapon stalks. They hit the truck but didn't stop it. The truck hit the Daleks, sending some careening in circles to either side of the street and crushing others beneath its ten wheels. Before it exploded.

Adelaide heard Julie and Adya gasp with horror and knew her own hand was planted over her mouth. But they had to move quickly. Maybe the explosion would keep the Daleks distracted long enough for them to get to their homes safely.

If there was such a thing as safe any more.

They moved quickly, keeping to the darkest parts of the streets, and keeping quiet. Distantly, there was still the sound of gunfire, soldiers were taking the fight to the strange invaders, but she heard only human screams. The Daleks, she thought, were like tanks, swiftly gliding tanks. She wasn't sure how much good bullets would be against tanks.

They got to Julie's house first. It was dark, but when she tapped on the door and called out nervously, the door opened and she was swallowed up in her mother's arms. Adya lived only four houses down, and her older sister was keeping watch from an upstairs window. By the time they got there the door was open. Adya's family begged Adelaide to come in, too, but she was determined to get to her own mum and dad.

She lived two streets away; it would take her no more than a minute. But as she slipped through the darkness at the end of Adya's road, a shape came out of nowhere and grabbed her.

'Adelaide!'

It was her father, tearful and terrified and thanking the god he had never believed in. He held her tight, and she clung to him, the tears she had refused to cry before finally breaking through.

She might have been ten years old, and practically an adult, like Julie had said, but he picked her up and carried her quickly back to their house. Like most of the others it was dark. And empty.

'Where's Mum?'

Dad told her he didn't know. He had been looking for her when he found Adelaide. Saturday mornings she always went to the gym. That was where she had been when things had gone crazy. No phones were working. All he could do was look for her. He had hoped that Adelaide would be safer out in the country, but he was still relieved to see her. Now, though, he was going back out again to find her mum. He told Adelaide to stay there in the house, and he'd be back soon

Adelaide didn't want him to go, but she wanted her mum back. She wanted them all together. The way they had used to be. Whatever had been the cause of their fighting, her dad still loved her mum, and Adelaide loved them both. But she would never see either one of them again.

Throughout the hours that followed, Adelaide heard sounds of fighting across the town, other explosions like the one that had destroyed the flower truck and, occasionally, the electronic bark of the Daleks. Eventually she had gone to her room and hidden herself without thinking about it in a corner.

Then, through the window across the room, she had seen the Daleks in the air. She'd had no idea that they could fly when she saw them on Chiswick High Road. Yes, they had glided across the ground, but fly?

They moved over the house roofs like big metal bugs without wings. No doubt in search of more humans to round up. She tried not to think about what they might be doing with them – and whether they had already captured her mother and, now, father. But the sight of the aerial Daleks was hard to resist, and she drew closer to the window.

Which, as if it had all been a plan to catch her, was when another Dalek rose up from below the bedroom window. The top of its head swivelled around and the long stalk with what was unmistakably some kind of eye fixed on her. She was powerless to move; exhausted and scared – and fascinated – she watched the Dalek as it watched her.

She had no idea how long they remained like that, and she felt tears gather in her eyes. Not because she thought the Dalek would attack. Somehow, then, it didn't matter if it did. Amid all that day's strangeness and fear, and the carnage that the Daleks had now brought with them, Adelaide felt touched by a moment in time.

Then, it stopped looking and flew away over the rooftops.

*

'That was it,' Adelaide told the Doctor. 'I swear it looked right into me, and then it simply went away.' With her finger she wiped away the tears that had again gathered in her eyes. 'And I knew. That night. I knew that I would follow it out there, into space.'

'But not for revenge,' the Doctor said.

She almost smiled. 'What would be the point of that?'

The Doctor's grin was more certain. 'That's what makes you remarkable. That's how you create history.'

'You mean Bowie Base One?' she asked doubtfully. 'Not a very successful part of history is it, now?'

But he wasn't done. 'Imagine it, Adelaide,' he said quietly. 'What if you begin a journey that takes the human race all the way out to the stars? Imagine, it begins with you, and then your granddaughter.'

Adelaide listened, watching the fires dance in his dark eyes.

'You inspire her. So that in thirty years' time Suzie Fontana-Brooke is the pilot of the first lightspeed ship to Proxima Centauri. And then – everywhere! With her children and her children's children forging the way to the Dragon Star, the Celestial Belt of the Winter Queen, discovering the Map of the Watersnake Wormholes.

'One day a Brooke will even fall in love with a Tandoonian prince, and that's the start of a whole new species! But everything starts with you, Adelaide. From fifty years ago, to right here. Today. Imagine.'

She stared at him, thinking about every word he had just said.

'Who are you?' she breathed.

He just looked at her, like he didn't have an answer she would believe.

'Why are you telling me this?

He drew in a breath. 'As consolation.'

Her mouth began to form a question, one that he knew he couldn't answer. But Adelaide's computer got there first with a beep that stole her attention.

'Andy Stone. He logged on yesterday with a report.'

Her fingers worked briefly over the keyboard and the monitor screen lit up with the young professor as he had been before the Flood. A good-looking man who enjoyed a laugh and could shrug off a minor annoyance like this one.

'Number Three water filter's up the creek. And guess what? The spares they sent don't fit. Big surprise! Anyway, no panic. One and Two filters are still working fine.'

Adelaide was checking the time code on the log: 21.20.

'That means the infection started today in the biodome. It's a week before water gets cycled out of there. So we're clear, the rest of the crew can't be infected.' She felt relief surge through her and smiled at the Doctor.

'We *can* leave!' She got on her comms. 'Ed, we're clear! We can proceed to launch. How are you doing?'

In the control room, Ed worked purposefully at his console to prep the take-off amid borderline chaos as the rest of the crew hurriedly loaded equipment and supplies onto trollies and ferried them to the shuttle launch pad.

'The shuttle is active, Captain,' Ed reported. 'Stage One. But if you want to eat for the next seven months we're going to have to carry it or go hungry.'

'I'm up for a picnic,' Adelaide told him, the relief showing in her voice.

'I'll make sure we've got scones,' Ed told her and closed off the transmission.

The Doctor leaned against the monitors, looking at Adelaide. 'So, the launch is go.'

'There's nothing to stop us now.'

The Doctor took off his glasses and looked down at his training shoes. He wasn't so sure about that.

But Adelaide had something else on her mind. 'Before we go, Doctor, there's something I want you to see.'

Chapter 10

Ancient History

Adelaide led the Doctor to a vault back in the Central Dome that wouldn't have been out of place at Fort Knox. Its door was heavier even than the airlock that was currently keeping the Flood at bay. If it, and its twin airlock at the biodome, were intended to preserve the base in the event of a depressurisation emergency, whatever they had in the vault had to be pretty special.

The Doctor had been given no clues during their journey to the vault. Adelaide had simply said that it was best he see for himself. Whatever it might be, it was a part of the Bowie Base One story that the Doctor had never heard. He felt excitement buzz through him like electricity as Adelaide entered a code and then hauled on the big wheel that opened the vault door.

The vault itself was not large. It had no reason to be, for what it guarded stood on a table in the middle, protected by a cylinder of glass. There was a single chair at the table and a computer terminal that he guessed was part of trying to unlock the artefact's secrets.

'It was found during the ice field excavation,' she explained, standing aside in the vault doorway for the Doctor to go take a look at Bowie's most prized discovery. 'As you know, the base was built by construction drones. It was sheer luck that this was spotted by a controller on Earth. Otherwise, it would probably have been destroyed without us ever knowing of its existence.'

The Doctor felt his breath catch in his throat as he approached the protective cylinder and began to realise what it contained. 'It wasn't taken back to Earth?' he said.

'The construction drones weren't designed to return to Earth. Mission Control decided it was best left here for us to examine when we reached Mars. Besides, they weren't sure it would survive the G-forces of a flight to Earth.'

'The Secret of Bowie Base One,' the Doctor marvelled, leaning gently on the table.

It was a three-sided column. Not solid. Constructed of three paper-thin sheets of delicate metal that stood just under a metre tall within the protective cylinder. Its surface glittered with a sheen of colours that seemed to move and change as he used the revolving plinth on which it stood to inspect each side in turn. The column was covered in an elaborate small script that reminded him of Nordic runes, but without their order.

'Who's the translator?' he asked.

'Mia.'

The Doctor nodded, smiling. 'I didn't think she was really a geologist. Her hands are too soft.'

'The Space Agency thought having a translation expert on the manifest would cause too many questions.'

'Has she got very far?'

'It's a long process.'

The Doctor dug out his spectacles again. The writing didn't run in straight lines, either vertical or horizontal, but in winding intricate spiralling patterns. He smiled. For such an uncompromising race, whose evolution had been so militaristic that its young were born into troops, not families, the Ice Warriors had one of the most beautifully decorative languages in the universe.

'It's beautiful, isn't it?' Adelaide said, now standing at his side.

'It's fabulous,' he said, both overjoyed and saddened.

'You see, we had made one of the greatest discoveries in history, even before we set foot on Mars. Proof that intelligent life had existed here.'

The Doctor nodded. 'And now that proof will be lost again.'

'It will remain here,' Adelaide agreed, misunderstanding him. 'But humans will return to Mars one day, prepared for the Flood. Humanity will unlock its secrets.'

No, thought the Doctor. It would be destroyed in the nuclear blast that would wipe out any trace that Bowie Base One ever existed. But as his eyes followed the currents of the ancient writing, his mood darkened further. 'If the Ice Warriors couldn't overcome the Flood, I doubt that humanity ever will.'

Adelaide's brow furrowed, 'What do you mean?'

He read to her from some of the last words ever written on Mars by its ancient natives:

I am Vazaal, Lord Prime Commander of my people. We have lived in the world of ice and snow for centuries since the magnetic storms that ravaged our planet. We are the last species of our once magnificent world that teemed with life of every kind in abundance. But now even we hardy people must flee this planet that we have loved, and I leave this warning to any future pioneers who might seek to explore what we leave behind. Beware, this world is cursed.

The ice that has given us shelter and succour for millennia, allowing us to rebuild our kind in the wake of our planet's long death, has turned against us. Its waters have brought upon us a contagion of hideous metamorphosis to which our armour and resolve are but frail leaves in resistance.

The Flood, for that is the name of this curse, came upon a meteor and found home in our waters and the ice that was once our salvation. No longer so.

For the life that lives within it now takes life and destroys it cell by cell, remaking it in its own hideous nature. An abomination of drowned flesh that cannot be destroyed. For who can destroy water?

In this way the Flood made an army of what were once our comrades, lovers, and children, turned by the touch of just a single drop of water, and then set this legion against us, to absorb us into its ranks.

We are warriors, we fear no enemy. But against water, we are powerless. All that we can do is render it inert as ice. But, that is no victory, for the water lies still and deep in the ground.

And so we leave our world to its long death and seek new planets for our people among the stars. And I leave you, future visitors, this warning: do not wake the waters.

The Doctor removed his glasses and tucked them away again. 'They tried to warn you, Adelaide, you just couldn't understand.'

She had listened to the Doctor read the ancient alien text that Mia had tried to crack for seventeen months without success, and she had accepted every word. Whoever this man was, and wherever he had come from, it didn't matter any more.

'If only you had got here sooner,' she said.

'Yeah,' he said, without conviction.

And she remembered what he had said beside the ice field: *What happens here must always happen.*

That was when Adelaide got the call on the comms: it was Steffi in the control room.

'Captain,' she said in a voice Adelaide had never heard her use before. Steffi was frightened. 'It's Maggie. She's got out of the isolation tank.'

Chapter 11

Water Calls

Yuri hadn't wanted to leave Maggie behind. Despite the changes, he had a hard time thinking of her as anything other than the mate with whom he had played endless rounds of kids' games in the rec room. She was one of the smartest people he had ever known – on paperwork the words *Maggie Cain* were followed around by more letters than most people had in their whole names – but she had brought a huge compendium of board games to Mars in her personal allowance. People sometimes thought that because he was Russian he had to be some kind of chess master; truth was Yuri enjoyed a game of Hungry Hippo way more. And Maggie had, too.

The thing she'd become hadn't moved the whole time that Yuri had been packing up medical supplies for the spaceflight home. She had remained with her hands pressed against the glass of the isolation tank, the water seeping out of her mouth and flesh, those strange, clouded eyes following him around. She had said nothing more since she spoke to the Doctor. Yuri was glad about that. That voice, like it was coming from the bottom of a stagnant pool of black water, sent icy spiders running up and down his back.

But finally he had all the meds he thought the crew could need during their seven-month journey back to Earth. They were all loaded on a trolley ready to go to the shuttle. Maggie remained in the same position, like a robot that had gone offline; only the eyes that tracked him across the room betrayed any sign of consciousness. It should have been easy for him to just close the door on her, but he could feel the pull on his heart. All those games they had played and all the laughs they'd had.

He imagined that she would die there, where she stood. Eventually. Alone in the silence and dark of the evacuated Mars base. And he wondered if there was a part of his friend still in there. Some part of her consciousness held captive by the Flood, unable to make herself known, but watching. There was a medical condition known as locked-in syndrome in which a person remained conscious whilst their entire body was paralysed. In the past, people had been buried alive like that. The idea of it had always frightened him. Maybe that was Maggie now. Dreading the moment when he turned off the light and closed the door. Yuri couldn't imagine how terrifying that would be.

There were enough drugs around him to put her out

of her misery before he left. But that would mean exposing himself to the Flood. Not a chance. He was going back to Earth and had already begun planning the life he would spend there with Mia.

'You understand, don't you, Maggie?' he said as he stood in the sickbay doorway. 'I'm sorry.'

He turned off the light and closed the door.

She stood in the darkness, although darkness did not exist for her.

The Flood were hydrogen and oxygen. They used her eyes, but sensing oxygen in the air and the forms around which it shaped was all they needed to see, whether it was light or dark.

She left the observation window where she had watched the flesh-being, waiting for him to leave. She moved to the isolation tank's door and set her hands on its frame. Water streamed through its structure, finding its weaknesses. The Flesh relied so much on electrical currents. They believed it kept them safe. But water vanquished electricity.

The door's electronic lock sparked and fizzed as the water seeped through it, rerouting the electrical charge and burning it out. The seals broke in a shower of victorious water and the door opened to the Maggie-thing's touch.

They had waited eons trapped in the ice below the planet's surface; waiting for the flesh-being to leave had been just the passing of a moment. But the creature took time to savour its release from the closed compartment in which it had taken full possession of this body. The air supply in the isolation tank had been separate to the air in the rest of the base. Now the water creature could feel the air that supplied the wider base and could hear on it the call of the Flood that came from the ice.

The creature raised the arms that had once belonged to Maggie Cain, tipped back its head, water flooding out of it and reabsorbing, and cried out.

The call of the Flood was a ghastly aqueous wail that reverberated through the air and walls of the Bowie base. It was picked up by the creatures outside the airlock that had once been Andy and Tarak, like wolves joining in the howling of their pack.

In the control room, the base crew, working frantically against the clock to be launch-ready, heard the ghastly sound and stopped whatever they were doing.

'What's that?' Mia asked, feeling her skin prickle with an unnatural cold.

'Nothing good,' Ed answered.

Steffi checked the isolation tank observation camera. Maggie was gone.

In the biodome tunnel, the two creatures that had joined in with the Maggie-thing's call abruptly stopped, just as she did. As if they had received instructions. As one, they turned and began to walk back towards the biodome and came to a large panel in the wall. It had handles. It came away easily.

Inside was a steel ladder.

Chapter 12

Leaving

When Adelaide got back to the control room with the Doctor, Steffi quickly brought her up to speed on their evacuation status. Ed, meanwhile, scrolled through the base cameras, looking for any sign of the Maggie creature. Yuri had delivered his medical supplies and was now helping Roman pack research equipment. Mia was executing downloads from the base data core.

The Doctor took it all in with admiration and a grieving sense of the futility of it all. He saw the Russian give Mia a reassuring smile and an OK sign, and she smiled back; he was telling her that everything was going to work out, they were going home, and they were going to be together.

None of that was going to happen.

The shuttle was ninety per cent prepped. Its ignition systems all checked out and the life-support analytics were almost complete. There was a red light showing on one of the carbon scrubbers that were part of the shuttle's air-recycling process, but Steffi reckoned they could fix that in-flight.

'It won't be an issue,' said Adelaide. 'We're lifting off three crew members light. I'm officially designating Andy, Tarak and Maggie as deceased—'

'I've got cameras going down all over Bowie,' Ed broke in.

Adelaide crossed to join him. 'Is it Maggie?'

'You can bet the farm on it. I've tracked for her all over the base. No sign. And . . .' He brought up the camera at the central dome airlock.

'Andy and Tarak. Where did they go?'

'No idea.'

Adelaide stiffened. 'We complete prep on the shuttle,' she said. 'Nothing else matters.'

'Yes, Captain.'

Adelaide turned back to the Doctor, who was standing like a spectre amid all the bustle of her crew. She collected his spacesuit from the locker where Steffi had stored it and presented it to him: 'I'm saving my people. Get back to your ship and save yourself, Doctor.'

The Doctor just looked at her. 'What about Andy and Tarak? And Maggie?'

'They can't get into the dome, and soon it won't matter. I know what this is, Doctor. It's the moment I save my crew, and we escape. You've done enough.'

The Doctor took the suit and helmet from her. Adelaide didn't waste time with goodbyes, she instantly turned back to her crew, helping move crates onto trolleys.

'Right, let's get this loaded! Roman!'

The young American steered the electric trolley through the door to the launch pad tunnel.

'On the double!' she shouted after him.

The Doctor took a step towards the door that would take him to the main external airlock and the Martian surface.

It was time to go.

But he stopped and took one last look at them, the crew of Bowie Base One. This was how he wanted to remember them, he thought: as determined and brave pioneers who had made a new world their home and showed humanity there was nothing it couldn't achieve if it worked together. He felt his eyes burning as he watched.

It was time to go. To leave them to their fate, to the headlines in a newspaper he had already read on a bench in New York, as the rain began to fall. To what had already happened and must always happen.

A light began to flash.

Just a small diode on one of the control panels. It made an insistent beeping sound.

Beeping sounds were never good. They got under your skin and picked at your nerves. They demanded to be noticed. They always brought bad news.

The Doctor waited.

And eventually, the beeping punctured the clamour of the evacuation preparations.

'What the hell is that noise?' Adelaide snapped.

Five seconds later, Ed had found the Andy and Tarak creatures: 'It's the module sensors. Exterior 12. The cameras are down but there's pressure on the module. Two signals.' He looked up at the ceiling. 'Right above us.'

'Andy and Tarak,' Adelaide breathed.

Steffi stared at the ceiling, 'They're on the roof. What can they be doing? How can they even be there?'

'Maintenance shafts,' Ed responded.

Mia shook her head. 'But how? The shafts are depressurised, and they don't have spacesuits.'

Adelaide glanced over to the Doctor, still standing by the door, the spectral witness to their battle for survival; he said nothing, and he didn't move. 'They breathe water,' she said. 'It's their environment. Their bodies generate it and they're covered in it. They might as well be wearing spacesuits.'

Adelaide Brooke, the Doctor thought, his hearts swelling as he stood by the door, *you could have been so magnificent*.

'But they still can't get through, can they?' Mia was asking. '*Can they?*'

Yuri reached out to hold her. 'We're safe, *dushen'ka*, this place is airtight.'

Steffi was grim. 'We didn't think Maggie could get out of the isolation tank. She still did.'

'Everybody!' Adelaide snapped, bringing back their focus as she pointed to the ceiling. 'That's ten feet of steel-combination up there. We've got time before we need worry, and we're using it to get off this planet!' She turned to Ed. 'Get to the shuttle and fire it up.'

'I can help load cargo,' he countered.

'That's an order!'

The Doctor watched Adelaide marshalling her crew as Roman returned from his trolley-run to the shuttle and Ed passed him in the other direction at a run, heading for the ship they thought would take them home.

The Doctor closed his eyes. It was time to put this behind him; there was nothing more he could do. He had fought in the Time War and survived the devastation of his own people; he had saved worlds and defended the sanctity of life in so many forms; when the Daleks had stolen Earth, he had returned it to its proper place and time. He had been the guardian of right in a chaotic but beautiful universe for so many lifetimes, and he had never in all those lifetimes felt so powerless.

He turned and left the control room.

Adelaide watched the Doctor slip away, saw the door close behind him.

And ten feet above her, on the other side of a layer of steel-combination that had been intended to resist the impact of meteors, the creatures that had taken possession of two of her crewmen got to their knees and spilled water over its surface. And microscopic imperfections in the dome's armour began to yield to the invasion of the water, drop by drop.

Chapter 13

Airlock

The Doctor pulled on his spacesuit and fitted the helmet. He twisted it ten degrees and felt the locks snap securely into place. Oxygen began to hiss quietly. The locking also brought the suit's communications online, and he could hear chatter from the Bowie control room. Ed had reached the shuttle and was running through the last ignition checks.

T-minus ten minutes.

There was relief in the crew's voices. For a moment, the Doctor could almost believe they were going to make it. That somehow there had been a glitch in the timeline and, this time, the crew of Bowie Base One would make it back to Earth. But he knew that was delusion.

He stepped into the airlock and pulled the inner door closed behind him. He moved to the outer door and tapped at the electronic lock that would automatically equalise the artificial base pressure with that of the surface and then release the locks. He would return to the TARDIS and take himself across the universe to wait for his song to end.

It is returning through the dark.

He will knock four times.

The airlock didn't open. The status panel read: LOCKED.

'Tell me what happens.'

Adelaide's voice was in his helmet.

There was a monitor over the airlock door. He saw her sitting alone in what looked like a screened alcove off the control room, her command station. Through the screen he could see Yuri and the others still working behind her, but the background chatter had been filtered out. There was just the two of them.

He looked her in the eyes and said, 'I don't know.'

'Yes, you do. Now tell me.'

'You should be with the others.'

'*Tell me!*'

The Doctor said nothing.

'I could make you tell me.'

He raised an eyebrow. 'You think so?'

'I have full control of the airlock from here. I could ramp up the pressure in there and crush you.'

'Except you won't,' he said. 'You could have shot Andy when we found him in the biodome, but you didn't. And I loved you for that.'

*

Damn him! At her command station, Adelaide glared at the spacesuited figure on the monitor screen. She had played the moment she had spared Andy Stone's life over in her head a dozen times since. She had been weak. She had been sentimental. She had seen her crewman there when he no longer existed. She should have fired the gun. Only . . . it wouldn't have made any difference, would it? They had already brought Maggie into the dome. Just as pursuing the Daleks for vengeance would have been meaningless, so, too, would have been shooting Andy, and Tarak. Just as being furious with the Doctor made no sense.

'All the same, Doctor, I need to know.'

Beyond the face-shield of his helmet she could see those dark sad eyes as he tried to find an answer for her.

'Imagine if . . . Imagine if you knew something . . .' he began, then faltered, and tried to find a better way . . . 'Imagine if you found yourself somewhere – I don't know – Pompeii . . . You were in Pompeii—'

'What the hell has that got to do with it?'

'You're in Pompeii the day Vesuvius erupts. August 25th, 79 AD. There are 2,000 people there. And you try to save them. But in doing so, you make it happen.'

'You're not making any sense.'

'Anything I do just makes it happen!'

Adelaide stared at him. The silence was like a chain wrapped around them both.

'Go on,' she said.

The Doctor closed his eyes and breathed deeply. The oxygen in his spacesuit tasted bitter. 'You're taking Action One,' he said. 'In the event of a mission failure crisis, there are four more standard action procedures.'

'You don't have to quote the base manual to me—'

'Action Five is—'

'Detonation.'

'The final option,' he said.

'But we're leaving . . .'

'Today, on November 21st, 2059, Captain Adelaide Brooke activates the self-destruct protocol on the nuclear reactor at the heart of Bowie Base One, taking the base and all her crew with her.'

He barely heard Adelaide's voice. 'No.'

'No one ever knows why. But you were saving Earth. When the investigation team arrives, the ice field has gone. Even water can't withstand a thermonuclear blast. The Flood has been destroyed.'

She was defiant. 'But we're taking the shuttle.'

'You never do.'

'We're doing it now!'

'You can't,' he said, and she could hear his voice break. 'No matter how hard you try, no matter what you do. You can't. It's what inspires your granddaughter. She takes the human race to the stars because you die on Mars.'

How could he know? How could he possibly know? And yet, she knew that he did.

'You die, Adelaide. Today. And Suzie flies out into the stars, like she's trying to meet you.'

No.

'I won't die. I will not.'

'Your death creates the future,' he said.

It was a wonderful epitaph. But she didn't want to die.

'Help me,' she said.

The Doctor didn't reply.

'This has to be why you're here,' she told him, and she could hear the desperation in her own voice. 'Wherever you come from, whoever you are, you have to be here today for a reason. And that has to be to help us survive.'

'I can't. I can't, Adelaide. I swear, I can't. I wish I could, believe me, but . . . no. Sometimes I can. Sometimes I do. Most times I can save someone, anyone. But not you.'

'My crew, then. Yuri, Mia. You can save them.'

'I can't help you.'

'Then I defy you, Doctor. I survived the Daleks. I will survive this!'

The Doctor reacted like he'd been scalded. 'You wondered all your life why the Dalek at your bedroom window didn't exterminate you,' he said. 'I think it looked at you and it knew your death was fixed in time for ever, just like that precise moment when it came over the rooftops to discover you and set the whole train of your life in motion. Time is a dance,

Adelaide, and we're all just following the melody until our turn on the floor is over.'

She stared at him. 'Then you'll die here, too.'

'No.'

'What's going to save you?'

'Captain Adelaide Brooke.'

They held each other's gaze for a moment that felt like forever. The screen was like a window – in it, she saw the Dalek that came to her the night her parents vanished.

She had heard the cries of people being exterminated by them. She had seen them attack Peter's flower truck as it bore down on them and exploded. She had never known why they had transported Earth light years across space, just as she had never known how the Daleks had been defeated, and Earth restored to its solar system. But she had known the Daleks were merciless killers. And yet this one had gazed at her as it hovered outside her room, and it had decided not to take her life.

The Dalek had understood her place in the dance and now she did, too.

Adelaide hit a button on her console and said, 'Damn you.'

The airlock door's electronic bolts released, and the Doctor was free to leave. She didn't watch him go. In the main control room area, people were screaming as water fell through the ceiling.

Chapter 14

Last of the Time Lords

Roman saw it before anyone else and at first thought it was his imagination. It was a single drop that was clinging to the edge of a white ceiling tile. But how could it be when there was a massive layer of steel above them? And then it fell. And Roman sprang backwards and looked back up at the ceiling as the droplet hit the floor.

'We've got water!' he yelled and saw that where the single bead had clung to the ceiling tile there was now a line of them, and more squeezing through on every side of the white square. 'Water!' he yelled again, moving further away, panicking, his head now swivelling around in every direction as he looked up.

There was water easing through between other tiles all over the control room.

'Don't let it touch you!' Yuri barked.

Steffi cried out for the captain as the droplets began to fall, at first like the first spots of rain in a summer shower, then faster, faster . . .

Adelaide lurched out of her command station and

saw water begin to pour through the ceiling and stream down the walls as Yuri, Roman, Mia and Steffi, pale with terror, dodged the showers as they broke through. She checked above her – there was no water showing yet.

'Get over here,' she yelled. 'For God's sake keep away from the water!'

Standing in the airlock, the Doctor heard the chaos erupting through the audio-feed in his helmet. Yells. Orders. Screams. Every sound drilling into him. Every cry another fracture in his hearts.

He heard Adelaide, desperate but defiant, order them to abandon the section. '*Yuri,*' he heard her command. '*Section B corridor. Lead the way!*'

Yuri gripped Mia's hand and opened the door to the corridor – and curtains of water fell ahead of him, solid sheets of water that denied any way through.

'It's no good,' he yelled, shifting back into the control room.

'Did it touch you?' Mia demanded, recoiling before she could stop herself, as Yuri got the door shut again.

'It's OK,' he told her in a level voice. 'I'm dry.'

In the airlock, the Doctor wondered just what it would take to break the big Russian's calm. In his head he could see the control room roof beginning to collapse around them as the water poured in.

*

'We'll have to take Section F. Go the long way around,' Adelaide commanded, carefully leading the way through rapidly shrinking dry pathways.

'What about the supplies?' Steffi shouted. 'The shuttle has only half the protein packs.'

'Carry what you can. After that, we go hungry! Come on!'

Yuri, Roman and Mia grabbed a bunch of silver packs and headed after Adelaide as tiles overhead began to burst, and columns of water spilled into the control room. But Adelaide's escape route was still dry. She turned back to see Steffi gathering tubes into her arms from one of the trollies. They were spare filters for the oxygen scrubbers, with one unit already down on the shuttle, they might need them. But they weren't worth the risk.

'Steffi, leave them!' Adelaide yelled.

There was a massive cracking sound above and a whole section of the ceiling finally fell in, creating a screen of water that divided the control room and cut Steffi off from the others.

'I'm trapped!' she screamed.

'Use the command station. Close the screen. We'll get to you through the wall panel!'

As Steffi scrambled to obey, behind Adelaide, Roman had got the Section F door open.

'It's clear this way!' he yelled.

*

Now inside the command station, Steffi backed away as water began to stream down on the other side of the glass screen. And tears glistened on her cheeks. She had always been a practical woman devoid of any trace of self-delusion. Miracles didn't happen; hope was something you based on reasoned fact. She was trapped, and she knew there was no way that Adelaide and the others were going to be able to get to her. Not in time. The glass screen wouldn't hold the water back for long, and the ceiling above her was just as likely to crack and open up the way it had across the rest of the control room.

She started to type into the computer, bringing up her personal call files. She opened the last video call she had received from her two girls back in Hamburg.

'Hallo, Mama.'

The Doctor heard their voices over the audio feed. Small girls, younger than Adelaide had been when she saw the Dalek. Not even eight years old, he thought. He couldn't imagine the wrench it must have been for Steffi to leave them behind when she went to Mars. She must have regretted it every day she had been there. He could hear her sobbing now, alone and trapped in a small room on a doomed Mars base as she listened and saw her children for the final time.

'I'm sorry, girls,' he heard her say. *'Lisette, Ulrika. God,*

I'm, so sorry.' And he heard her scream as the water finally broke through the ceiling and took her.

The Doctor couldn't bear any more. He opened the airlock door and stepped out onto the Martian surface. But there was no escape from the horrors that screamed in his space helmet.

'*Steffi?*' Adelaide was shouting, '*Steffi are you there? Can you hear me? For God's sake answer me, please!*'

In the control room the glass screen opened and, through the curtain of falling water, Adelaide could see a shape step out and draw closer. It looked like Steffi, but she knew that it wasn't, even before she saw the dead white eyes and the cracked skin seeping water from inside her.

'Out!' she commanded the others, though it sounded more like a disbelieving croak than an order. 'We've lost her. Everybody out!'

She closed the door on the control room and the water that now possessed Steffi.

The Doctor took long slow steps across the Martian surface as he heard Adelaide contact Ed. She and the others were running along the Section F corridor, they were going to have to take the long way to the launch pad, how was he doing? The Doctor turned and looked at the shuttle clamped to the gantry behind him; there was nothing sleek or elegant about it, not like some spacecraft he had seen. The shuttle looked like a piece of industrial hardware, burned at the nose by previous re-entries, and standing on four huge, charred rocket engines that were now beginning to smoke in the early stages of ignition.

Ed was sitting in one of the two pilot seats at the nose of the shuttle, effectively lying on his back as the rocket pointed at the sky. The flight deck was lit up with small bright diodes. A hundred or more instruments, all glowing and ready to launch.

'All systems online, Captain,' he told her. 'Don't you worry, this bird is gonna fly!'

'Affirmative,' Adelaide said, powering along the Section F corridor. 'We're two minutes from Launch Control. Stand by.' She turned to the others. Yuri and Mia were right behind her. Roman was further back down the corridor. 'Come on, now. We're almost there.'

Roman stopped.

'Roman, come on!'

Roman stood stock still. The others were less than twenty paces ahead of him. Less than twenty paces, and he could be with them. But no, he couldn't be.

'Roman!' the captain was shouting, urging him forward with one hand.

But Roman shook his head.

It had been a single drop.

He had only felt it, not seen it. But he had known what it was and what it meant. It had fallen from the ceiling and caught the side of his face. Cold, but it burned like fire.

'You'd better go without me,' Roman said.

Yuri and Mia turned together to look at him. 'Roman,' Yuri said, pain in his eyes. 'My friend, no. Please!'

But Roman couldn't answer. His skin was beginning to crack, his mouth blackened, and his body started to shake and jerk. He closed his eyes as it took him, as the icy water burst through his skin and poured from his hands.

'Out of here!' Adelaide snarled. 'Move!'

Together, she and Mia and Yuri ran for the next door – and they heard Roman coming after them, shrieking that unearthly, marsh-throated cry. As Yuri slammed the door on him, Adelaide caught just a glimpse of those awful corpse-like eyes. Roman hammered on the door. Yuri fused its lock, jamming it shut.

They paused and drew breath. *Another friend gone*, Adelaide thought. *Damn this base. Damn Mars.*

Then she led them through the last door into Launch Control. It was a circular chamber with all the tech to oversee launch and shuttle landings. It wasn't a big place and now it was crammed with crates that they had packed up for the evacuation but there hadn't been time to load onto the ship.

'We're going to make it,' Mia whispered.

'Ed! We're at Launch Control,' the Doctor heard Adelaide say over the comms.

But there was no immediate response.

'Ed? Report.'

'Sorry, Captain.' The Doctor heard the Australian's voice, strained and wretched. 'The shuttle is compromised.'

He closed his eyes. *They tried so hard. They fought, together, for survival, like the very best of humanity. But they could never win, even though they deserved to.*

'I heard someone ... climbing the ladder onto the flight deck. It was Maggie. I'm sorry, skipper. There was no time. There was so much bloody water.' Ed's breath was coming in sharp bursts. The Doctor could hear it in his voice: Ed was fighting the Flood. Fighting the change that he knew was coming in his body, every word a growing torture. 'They want this ship. They want to get to Earth. Can't let them do that.'

'Ed,' Adelaide said quietly. 'I'm so sorry.'

The Doctor sensed the Australian smile, though it quickly turned into a gasp of agony. 'Doesn't matter. We tried, didn't we? You know, I always hated this bloody job. You never gave me a chance, Adelaide.' He cried out; he was losing the fight. 'No couples,' he said. 'Good rule. Get your heads down . . . I'll see you later.'

This wasn't part of the newspaper story, just like the Flood wasn't, but the Doctor knew what was coming next, anyway. In his head he saw Ed reach for the ignition controls . . .

The shuttle erupted in a violent burst of raging energy that began at the rocket engines and ripped through the length of the craft in less than a heartbeat. Despite the thin Martian atmosphere, the Doctor felt the energy wave hit him like a truck and slam him to the ground, rolling him over and over in the dirt as burning fuel and debris showered down around him. In his helmet he heard Yuri, Mia and Adelaide scream as the explosion shook Launch Control. It was reinforced in the event of a launch accident. But that wouldn't save them from what was to come.

The Doctor finally found himself lying on his chest watching as a burning part of the fuselage flew towards him. It was part of the shuttle's nose cone, and it would weigh as much as the battered London bus that had once brought him and Carmen back to Earth from a planet covered in the dust of its dead. A part of him briefly wondered if this was how his song would end, that Adelaide had been right; that he would die here on Mars with the rest of them for refusing to help.

His thoughts flashed like sparks through his head in that split-second that felt like an eternity. When he'd confronted the Daleks after they stole Earth and twenty-six other planets in a plot to destroy reality, their creator Davros had taunted him. The Doctor never carried a gun, Davros had said, but he weaponised people. For a man who was supposed to care so much, he had used so many people, and in the process *lost* so many.

But always, the Doctor had told himself, to save lives. Always for the universal good. It hurt now because whoever he had saved – and sometimes that meant whole worlds – he couldn't save Adelaide and her crew. He burned with grief and regret.

He couldn't help. There were laws. Laws that governed Time and his place in it. Without them there would be chaos throughout every temporal dimension. He was a Time Lord – the last of the Time Lords – and he was all that guarded the gates from utter universal anarchy. To save Adelaide was to risk setting that anarchy loose.

The burning fuselage section flew right over him and crashed into the red Martian soil twenty metres away. The Doctor barely even flinched. Time knew when he was to die. Like the death of Adelaide Brooke, it was a fixed point and could never be amended.

Yet, the Doctor knew that *he* was a part of Time. The artron energy of the Time Vortex was just as much a part of a Time Lord and his TARDIS as it was the very flow of Time, itself. He was a part of Time, and Time was a part of him. That was his very nature, and the nature of his people. They had been inseparable from it. Only now his people were all gone, and he was alone. Alone in Time.

In his helmet he heard Yuri yelling. The blast from the exploding shuttle had damaged the dome shell. They were losing oxygen from Launch Control.

The Doctor slowly got to his knees, then planted a foot in the red soil and pushed himself to his full height. Around him the flames of the shuttle wreckage were beginning to die, starved of oxygen in the denuded Martian atmosphere. But he was alive. The last of his kind.

Time had saved him from the fate of his home world and its people, as he had brought the Time War with the Daleks to an end. He had grieved for his people and his part in their destruction over lifetimes ever since. But he had done what he'd had to. It was Time that had placed the means in his hands.

Time itself had made him the last of the Time Lords. It had dictated that he should live, as Gallifrey was destroyed.

It had relinquished itself to his guardianship, alone.

He had won the Time War and now he understood that his victory had been more than survival.

The Last of the Time Lords.

And he turned to walk back through the wreckage, back to Bowie Base One.

Chapter 15

The Doctor Returns

Launch Control was in chaos and the three surviving humans were exhausted and on the verge of breaking. They had fought so hard for their lives, but at every turn they had been denied victory. Nevertheless, they had never given up. But now a maelstrom of escaping atmosphere tore at their hair and clothes, and the smell of burning filled the thinning air as equipment damaged by the blast smouldered and sparked. The shuttle had been destroyed and with it their only hope of seeing Earth, or another day.

Adelaide was bent over the launch console. The smoke and the dwindling air made her chest heave painfully. She told herself that she would not give up, but her body was bruised and hurting, and there was another voice in her head that said maybe it was better to end like this. One of the symptoms of oxygen starvation, she knew, was an unnatural sense of euphoria and tiredness. As the oxygen escaped the dome, they would fall asleep and die happy. Better than falling prey to the Flood.

When she saw the Doctor standing there in his strange orange spacesuit, his helmet under his arm, she thought she was hallucinating. Maybe he had always been a hallucination.

But suddenly, briskly, he was ordering them into action. 'Mia, sealant! Get that breach in the roof fixed, now! Yuri, open the emergency oxygen . . .'

He was electrified, determined, undefeatable.

And now he was looking at her. 'Adelaide, don't just sit there!'

Mia had already grabbed the sealant gun from the glass-fronted emergency cabinet behind Adelaide and was stopping the atmosphere breach with ropes of thick, quick-setting polymer. Yuri was spinning the wheels on two pipes, opening a flow of fresh air into the chamber.

The rushing wind as oxygen escaped began to slow as the sealant hardened, and its sound was replaced by the gentle whispering of air coming in through the auxiliary pipes.

The Doctor helped Adelaide up and used a fire extinguisher to fix the smouldering equipment, then seemed to take in everybody's work like a road gang boss proud of his team's effort: 'That's better! Well done, everyone! The dome's still got integrity. That's ten feet of steel-combination up there! Made in Liverpool! Magnificent workmanship!'

There was a light burning in his eyes that Adelaide

hadn't seen before. It was a new determination. He had come back, no longer a passive spectator. Now, he had joined their fight. Maybe there was hope after all.

Why, then, was she disturbed and not comforted?

Quietly, so that the others wouldn't hear, she asked, 'Why have you come back?'

He smiled at her, 'Because you need me. I'm the Doctor. Help is my middle name. What I do. Always. Without fail.'

She drew closer to him, her voice even quieter. 'You told me, it can't be stopped. Don't die here with us.'

He was almost laughing. 'Don't worry. Someone told me just recently – they said I was going to die. They said, *He will knock four times*. That's why I came to Mars in the first place! A bit of peace and quiet to think on that. Cos when someone tells you that you're gonna die you want to process it and prepare for it. Right? Anyway – no peace, no quiet.'

'You found us,' she said. He reminded her of a hyperactive child, full of energy looking for somewhere to blow it all.

'Yeah. So, *he will knock four times*. I think I know what that means, you see? And it doesn't mean right here, right now. Cos I don't hear anybody knocking, do you?'

Slam!

They all turned like they'd been pulled on a line.

Someone – *something* – was on the other side of the

door. Maybe it was Roman. Maybe it was all of them out there, trying to get in.

Slam!

Whoever – whatever – it was, they were hitting the door with the force of a jackhammer. They could see depressions pushing through the steel with each blow.

Slam!

The Doctor was fast on his feet. 'Three knocks is all you're getting!'

Adelaide saw he had what he called his screwdriver in his hand again as he did something to the pressure pad on the wall that operated the door. For one horrible moment she thought he was going to open it – let in the Flood, allow them to finish the job they had started with Andy and then Maggie. But when he hit the mechanism the door glowed and crackled with electricity and the next time whatever was out there tried to get in, it cried out in agony. It was a strange, shrill shriek that reminded her of steam escaping an old kettle with a whistle.

'Water and electricity, never a good combination,' the Doctor proclaimed triumphantly. 'And the Flood don't like it when it zaps back! Oh, they can fuse circuits, but hit them with a few thousand volts, and they're poached!'

Across Launch Control, Adelaide saw Yuri and Mia smile and glance at each other. The Doctor had returned, and he had brought them hope that they still might live. But she had heard his words in the airlock.

Their death was a fixed point in time, and he couldn't do anything about that. No one could.

They all listened. No other sound came from beyond the door. The Doctor hadn't killed it, he said, but he had seen it off for now.

'So we can use electricity against them,' Yuri said with new confidence.

'Yeah. But it won't stop them for good. And with all that water everywhere it's as dangerous for us as it is for them. So what else have we got? Eh? What's really bad news for water?' He was prowling around the room, his eyes alight, his body zinging with energy. 'Heat! Yes, heat's good! They're made of water so we can use heat! Worked against the Ice Warriors on the Moon. It can work against the Flood. I can ramp up the environmental controls, boost the temperature across the base. Might get a bit equatorial in here. But we can heat things up – and steam them! Whaddya say, Team Bowie?'

Yuri was beaming and looking at Mia as much as the Doctor. 'Sounds like a good plan!'

The Doctor grinned with a glee that was almost savage, 'Let's turn it up to Gas Mark Eight.' Like a gymnast, he leaped over one of the launch-control units and got busy hacking the base environmental systems.

Adelaide joined him there, confused and concerned. 'You said that we die. For the future. For the human race.'

He barely looked up from what he was doing, hitting buttons and spinning dials in a frenzy, like he was playing some kind of wild fairground game. 'Yes,' he said. 'Because there are laws. Laws of Time. And, you know, once upon a time there were people in charge of those laws. Time Lords, like me. But they all died. And guess who that leaves?'

Now he looked at her and she saw his eyes, that had once been so dark and sad, blazing with a triumphal glory.

'Me!' the Doctor said.

Adelaide felt like she wanted to back away. This wasn't the man she had spoken to in the airlock, the man that had been so sorry that he had to leave them to die. She had seen the pain in his eyes then. She had sensed the tortured emotions that he felt. This was a man that had somehow been reborn out on the Martian surface and had returned to them transformed, just as the Flood had transformed her crew and, somehow, just as dangerous.

'It's taken me all this time, Adelaide, more time than you could believe, all this time to understand. The Time Lords are gone, and so the Laws of Time are mine! *And they will obey me!*'

Adelaide felt her spine turn to ice.

Then she and the Doctor were thrown across the room as the control panel exploded. Yuri rushed in with the fire extinguisher as the Doctor regained his feet and helped Adelaide up.

'Looks to me like Time has got other ideas, Doctor.'

'No!' he snapped back. 'Not beaten yet! I'll go outside and use a heat regulator!' But as he reached for his helmet he saw the faceplate had been smashed. He had left it on the console when he set to work on the environmental settings. The blast had left it useless. He studied the damage grimly.

Time and Time Lord at war.

He passed the sonic screwdriver over the control panel looking for a reason for the explosion. But it was Mia, at a monitor on the other side of the room that gave him his answer.

'The Flood – they're doing something to the glacier!'

The ice field was a fundamental element of Bowie's environmental balance. Whatever the Flood were up to down there it had had a cataclysmic effect on the base habitat protocols.

'Doesn't matter! Doesn't matter!' the Doctor barked, more to himself than anybody else, pacing the length of Launch Control. 'Not beaten! Not beaten! You've got spacesuits in the next section!'

He lurched for the door to the neighbouring area, it opened on a corridor awash with water, more streaming down the walls. Horrified, he slammed the door shut again.

'We're not just fighting the Flood,' he said. 'We're fighting Time itself!'

Yuri and Mia exchanged an anxious glance. Was this what it was like to watch a man lose his mind?

'Doesn't matter!' he yelled again, out loud, like he was challenging the universe and all of reality. 'I'm gonna win.'

'Doctor . . .' It was Adelaide stepping forward, like a parent concerned for her child. She reached toward him, not sure if she was going to hug him or slap him.

But the Doctor spun himself around, pulling on his hair, beating his head with his fists. '*Thinkthinkthink!*' His wild eyes searched the room as his racing thoughts spilled out as words. 'What have we got? What have we got?

'Not enough oxygen!

'Protein packs? Useless!

'Spare parts! Electric carts!

'Glacier! Glacier!

'Minty?

'Minty!

'Glacier minty?

'Minty? Monty?

'*Molto bene!*

'Bunny, bonny!

'Bish-bash-bosh-baaaaaaaaah!

'The room! Look at the room!' The Doctor stopped turning, cocked his head. 'What have we got? Boxes, crates. What we got in the box?'

'It's just storage,' Yuri told him.

'What storage?'

'I don't know. Stuff we weren't taking with us. Weather spikes. Atom clamps . . .'

The Doctor was already pulling the crates and boxes open. Like a frenzied kid on Christmas morning. 'Atom clamps?' He almost sang it. 'Who needs atom clamps?'

And then he had another crate open, and his face split into the biggest smile.

'Oh, I *love* a funny robot!'

Chapter 16

The Flood Rises

The creature that had once been astrobiologist Maggie Cain understood that it had made a mistake. It had underestimated the strength of the flesh-creature aboard the spacecraft.

Their occupation of the first bodies they had taken since their awakening had been easy and quick; even in this body where they had purposefully delayed the physical signs of their presence as part of their strategy of possession. But the dormancy of the Flood had been long and dark, and the Flesh on this world now was unlike the last that had lived there. That Flesh had been cold-blooded and physically superior to the warm-blooded Flesh they now took. But mentally the cold-bloods had been accustomed to existence as an element of a greater body. They had been armed and armoured, but their sense of belonging to cohorts and troops had made their subjugation almost flawlessly simple. They had assumed the warm-blooded Flesh would succumb just as easily. In the spacecraft they had been proved wrong.

They had intended to take the flesh-being but preserve enough of its knowledge to carry them across space to the beautiful planet of water and flesh they called Earth. But the flesh-creature had resisted their invasion of its cellular construction. Even though it must have felt its body succumbing to their touch, cell by cell, and known it was impossible to overcome their occupation, it had battled against them. It could never succeed, but it had resisted long enough to destroy itself and the ship that would have taken them to Earth and its sparkling waters.

The Flood that inhabited Maggie's body had recognised the miscalculation and had escaped the spacecraft before the Flesh had destroyed it.

Returning to the creatures' habitat, it had found other Flesh now occupied by the Flood but wandering through the now waterlogged corridors and chambers like purposeless wraiths. The remaining Flesh had sealed itself into a dry part of the habitat and had defended itself from their advance with electrical energy. The Flood would eventually reach them, because water never tired, never aged, and would wear away any wall the Flesh chose to hide behind. But Flesh did tire and did die. And if there was another way of reaching Earth, the Flood might not have time to find it before the flesh-beings were overtaken by their own bodily decay.

They could sleep again, of course. But they had slept

too long, and they yearned to join with the blue waters of Earth.

Using the creature that had been Maggie, the Flood called its walking elements together. Her cry was loud, long and mournful: a wail from the bottom of a cruel ocean of storms and death. The other bodies now possessed by its waters answered with their own aqueous howling chorus. As one, they all made their way through the devastated, drowned base to the ice field.

They felt the presence of their kind growing stronger the closer they drew to the frozen subterranean reservoir, the voices of the Flood called out to them from their mass hibernation in the ice. Millions of them, billions within the glacier of untold mass.

The flooded bodies assembled on the steel platform that overlooked the ice field. The corporeal entities that had belonged to Andy Stone, Taruk Itul, Roman Groom, Steffi Ehrlich and Maggie Cain. Although consumed by the Flood, each still retained imprints of their previous existence and it was those of the senior technician that the Flood chose to use now as she moved across to the spread of control panels on the platform.

The others, water spilling from their bodies, raised their arms and began to call to their kin still held by the frozen waters of Mars. It was a strange song, like the crashing of waves and the whirling cry of typhoons whipping an ocean into frenzy.

The Steffi creature did not sing. She worked calmly

and quickly at the environmental controls. In some other part of the base, she could see, one of the Flesh was also trying to manipulate the habitation protocols. She took care of that with an activation code that destroyed the peripheral they were using, then continued with her own work on the Bowie pressure protocols.

The air pressure in which the Flesh lived beneath their domes was artificial. It was kept that way to make the habitat comfortable for their bodies of meat and bone. At the bottom of their oceans on Earth the pressure would crush them. The environmental controls she now operated could increase the artificial pressure under the domes to crush the Flesh without harming the Flood. But the Flood did not want to crush them. The Flood wanted to be free. And reducing the atmospheric pressure within the domes would do that.

As the other flooded bodies sang to their kindred, the ice began to crack. Tiny spreading fractures that then broke into deep yawning fissures that began to break the vast glacier apart. They were raising the Flood.

There were countless tons of ice in the subterranean reservoir. An incalculable mass that, as it cracked, would turn to water and, as the base pressure became unstable, would shoot out of the cavern and wash through the entire base, ultimately surging like an ocean through corridors, no door able to withstand its crushing velocity.

Chapter 17

Gadget

Adelaide had a headache. It felt like the last thing she needed right now. The last couple of hours had been killers, and the Doctor's return to the base, pumped up with a new bravura and unrelenting determination to overcome what he had earlier claimed was both inevitable and invincible, wasn't helping. At the same time, she knew that didn't really make sense: she had quietly pleaded with him to help them all; he had refused, and then returned with a maniacal conviction that he could defeat fabled forces of the entire universe to ensure they lived. Nothing made sense to her any more.

Across Launch Control, he had wheeled Gadget out of its crate and was working in a frenzy of energy to set up Roman's operations console for the robot and prep it for whatever plan he now had. She couldn't make up her mind – was he the heroic genius that might just save them, whatever he had earlier claimed that Time decreed – or was he just a lunatic? She wondered how a lunatic could possibly have made it to Mars.

Pain lanced through her head like a hot stiletto behind her eyes. She felt sick, too.

Across the room Mia was checking her emergency repairs to the rupture in the roof. She suddenly stumbled and almost fell, but for Yuri catching her. 'Hey, are you OK?' he asked.

Adelaide was on her feet, joining them, a new worry taking shape in her head as she heard Mia complain that she, too, had a headache and felt sick.

'Hypobaric hypoxia,' she said, helping him with Mia, who looked dazed and weak. Headaches, fatigue and nausea were among the first symptoms of what climbers called altitude sickness.

The Doctor looked up from Gadget suddenly. 'The Flood are meddling with Bowie's atmospheric pressure. Well, you didn't expect them to give up, did you? We're not!'

'But what are they doing, Doctor?'

'They're down on the ice field. My guess is they're waking the rest of their kind. Lower the atmospheric pressure enough and the ice turns to water – then, the water shoots out of there like a geyser. They're going to flood Bowie Base!'

'My God,' Adelaide gasped. 'What are we going to do?'

'Send Gadget to the rescue,' he grinned.

'*Gadget-Gadget!*' said the robot.

Adelaide turned away in despair. *Madness!*

She didn't see him hand the robot something small and silver.

'You take care of that, now,' the Doctor said. 'There's a good Gadget. Now, off we go!'

She sat down at the launch console and looked back. The Doctor was wearing Roman's remote-action gloves that controlled the robot, and Gadget was heading for the door to the neighbouring section.

'Go boy! Go!' the Doctor was yelling, like a man with a bet on a horse. Adelaide wasn't giving him good odds.

The door opened, and there was the momentary sound of cascading water out in the corridor beyond.

'*Gadget-Gadget!*' Then Gadget was gone and the door closed behind him.

On Roman's screen, the Doctor watched as the robot progressed through the passageway. He used the gloves to guide it round obstacles and through gathering pools of water. Gadget's body had been sealed to keep out the fine Martian dust that had in the past clogged up and wrecked early surface probes. It kept Gadget's circuitry safe from water.

Far below, on the platform above the ice field, the flooded bodies of Adelaide's crewmembers stood with their arms raised like celebrants, their strange song still gurgling in their throats. Below the staging, blocks of blue-white ice were beginning to rise free from the glacier, their edges starting to drip, and drip.

And, in Launch Control, Adelaide turned to the keyboard before her and started to type activation codes. The screen pulsed with colour four times. Then there were two words:

ACTION FIVE

Gadget had reached an external airlock. The Doctor guided it through the opening procedure and silently thanked Roman for having given the robot such dextrous hands. The mechanical fingers punched in the airlock passcodes and moments later Gadget trundled inside.

As he waited for the airlock to pressure-equalise with the surface, the Doctor glanced across the control room at Adelaide. She was sitting motionless at the launch console. He couldn't see what she was looking at. He could sense the atmospheric pressure changing in the base, but it wasn't at any catastrophic tipping point yet. When it hit that, the entire base would flood in seconds. Gadget was going to have to move fast.

He saw the airlock had stabilised with the surface environment. Gadget opened the external door, and its tracks took it down onto the Martian dirt.

'Now,' he said. 'Let's get moving!'

He engaged the robot's boosters he had first used to escape the Flood outside the biodome. On the Launch Control external camera feed, the Doctor saw Gadget once again leave a trail of burning soil as it rushed away from the base.

'Look at it go!' Yuri marvelled. 'Like a comet on wheels!'

Adelaide didn't look up from the screen before her. Something about her sitting there, unmoving, disturbed the Doctor. 'Adelaide, what are you doing?'

She didn't respond. Simply typed something and hit return.

The Doctor was busy guiding Gadget across the surface at the speed of a Hyperiax rocket racer, so he couldn't afford to break off, no matter what Adelaide might be up to. He called across to Mia and told her to check it out for him.

Adelaide did nothing to hide what she had done as Mia joined her at the console. Mia clapped a hand across her mouth in shock as she saw the words on the screen.

ACTION FIVE ACTIVATED.

'Oh my God,' Mia gasped. 'Action Five!'

On screen, the self-destruct countdown had begun.

100

99

Adelaide turned to the stunned Mia and Yuri. 'I'm sorry. It's what we have to do.'

The Doctor burned with fury. 'Adelaide, if I have to fight you as well, I will!'

He turned back to Gadget's viewscreen, and punched forward with his gloved fists.

'Fasterrrrrrrr!'

On the surface of Mars, the sand beneath the robot's tracks no longer burned, but glowed white and fused into glass as Gadget accelerated even further.

In the glacial cavern beneath the crust, the flooded bodies sang louder, and rising blocks of ice the size of houses began to vibrate and explode into water.

In Launch Control everything began to shake violently.

'What's that, an earthquake?'

'No, Yuri,' the Doctor yelled back over the building rumble and shaking. 'It's an ice-quake!'

83

82

81

Suddenly Mia snatched the pulse pistol from Adelaide's belt. She couldn't believe she was doing it, but she was. The gun was aimed right at her captain.

'Disarm it!' she said. 'Now!'

Controlled, Adelaide took a languid look along the length of the gun and focused on Mia. On her terrified face.

For the first time since this nightmare had begun, Adelaide felt at peace with everything that had happened, and what was going to happen, and what would come to pass because of it.

'*No matter how hard you try, no matter what you do . . . It's what inspires your granddaughter. She takes the human race to the stars because you die on Mars . . .*'

'I can't disarm it,' Adelaide told Mia.

The Doctor was rigidly focused on Gadget's viewscreen as Launch Control continued to shake. It felt like the whole structure was in danger of coming apart.

Suddenly, Yuri was shouting: 'Oxygen breach!'

The shaking had torn open Mia's emergency fix and air was once again being sucked out as a storm of decompression tore at their hair and clothes.

The Doctor saw Yuri grab the sealant gun, trying to pack the breach. Then he finally saw what he'd been waiting for on Gadget's view screen. In the distance, standing alone in the red desert, the TARDIS.

'Yes!' he yelled, exultant.

73
72

Mia still held the gun on Adelaide, though her hands were trembling, 'Disarm it, Captain! Please . . .'

Adelaide spoke softly: 'Do you really think that killing me will make any difference?'

68
67
66

Of course, it wouldn't. Mia could see Yuri desperately trying to patch the atmosphere leak as the growing storm of escaping oxygen roared around them, and Launch Control trembled violently. She could smell burning now, and saw that a couple of damaged control panels had flames licking out from within; while the Doctor danced like some kind of crazed witchdoctor as he operated Gadget. It was getting harder to breathe and her vision was starting to blur.

Mia knew with horrid certainty that they were all going to die here.

She lowered the pistol. Adelaide took it and caught Mia as the next shockwave almost took them to the floor.

*

Out on the surface, Gadget now stood outside the TARDIS and produced the small silver object the Doctor had told it to take care of.

At Bowie Base One, the Doctor watched the screen and carefully mimed putting the key into the TARDIS lock and turning it.

'Yes! And we're in!'

60

The police box doors swung open and Gadget swept up the ramp toward the console.

'*Gadget-Gadget!*'

'Yes, well, we're not there yet,' the Doctor breathed.

Around him the world was in chaos. Smoke filled the thinning air. Yuri had sunk to his knees to hold Mia who was now barely conscious. Adelaide stared at the countdown.

55
54
53

Far below them the ice field was dissolving, replaced by a furiously spinning tornado of water that sucked up more and more of the thaw as it rotated wildly.

On the staging, the flooded bodies held their arms

aloft, singing and bathed in the wash thrown by the huge waterspout, welcoming their kin as they spilled over them, awoken from their ancient hibernation in a violent, victorious, storm.

After eons of dormancy, the waters of Mars raged and rejoiced.

29
28
27

Gadget was at the TARDIS console now, flicking switches under the Doctor's remote guidance, twisting dials and pulling levers. Between them, they had to get this right. The temporal displacement had to be perfect.

The rotor at the heart of the TARDIS console began to move, pumping up and down.

Up and down.

14
13
12

The Doctor heard his ship's ancient engines begin to wail and roar.

Across the room, Yuri was holding the unconscious

Mia to his chest as the oxygen ran out and Adelaide looked across at the Doctor. He was finally still.

But he was smiling.

3

2

1

Chapter 18

Time Lord Victorious

At 21.52 hours Mission Time on Friday 21 November 2059, Bowie Base One, the first permanent human outpost on Mars, was destroyed by a nuclear blast.

Giovani 3, one of the survey satellites that had orbited the Red Planet since the first days of planning for the Bowie mission and had helped select its location in the Gusev Crater, captured the explosion in a series of high definition pictures that were immediately transmitted to Earth. They showed the brief nuclear plume in graphic detail. The atomic flash and superheated cloud of gas and debris that followed lasted only 5.7 seconds in the weak Martian atmosphere.

Successive pictures by Giovani 3 showed that where the multi-domed base had been only seconds before there was now only a blackened depression of Martian regolith fused into glass by the heat of the detonation. Analysis of the automatic datastream from Bowie Base One would eventually show that the explosion was the result of emergency protocol Action Five, the outpost's self-destruct procedure, being triggered by Captain Adelaide Brooke.

But.

Ten seconds after the nuclear blast, before Giovani 3's photographs had been transmitted, and therefore before Mission Control could know the base had been destroyed, a strange industrial wheezing and grinding sound began in a quiet night-time street not far from where Hammersmith Bridge crossed the River Thames. Nobody heard the sound; it was snowing in London that night and nobody was out in the cold weather to see the old police box that materialised among the Victorian townhouses that ran along the street, as the strange noise died away.

The police box door opened and the Doctor stepped out, joyous as he felt snowflakes settle in his hair. 'Oh, snow! I love snow!'

He had discarded the orange spacesuit, and now pulled on an overcoat that hung down almost to his ankles and the trainers that crunched in the freshly fallen snow, as he breathed in the winter air. He swung back towards the TARDIS with an air of expectation as Adelaide, Yuri and Mia emerged, all confused. All more fearful than he thought they had a right to be. After all, hadn't he just saved them all?

He stood in the snow and challenged them: 'Isn't anyone going to thank me?'

They looked at each other and looked around them, shivered in the November air, and didn't know what to say.

'*Gadget-Gadget!*' The robot followed its crewmates out of the TARDIS, left a few feet of track-marks in the snow and abruptly stopped, its diodes going dark.

'Lost his signal, doesn't know where he is,' the Doctor observed, almost sad to see Gadget die. 'Don't you get it?' he suddenly demanded, turning on his passengers, his rescued souls. 'This is November 21st 2059! It's the same day. On Earth. I've brought you all home!'

He knew humans could be a confusing species, but this lot took the biscuit. *They took the whole jar!* The Doctor stretched out his arms and turned his face into the falling snow; it gathered in his hair, on his features and in his hands. 'You don't have to be scared any more! It's just frozen water, and that's all it is! Who wants a snowball fight?'

But he saw Mia staring at him as she held on to Yuri's hand, as if she was scared he might fly off like a balloon in a storm if she didn't; or maybe frightened that her sanity already had. '*Who are you?*' she asked in a voice that trembled. 'And what the hell is *that*?'

She was looking back at the TARDIS. The door was open, and she could still see its interior stretching way back, and in every dimension, far beyond the confines of its exterior.

'I know,' the Doctor said. 'Bigger on the inside. Don't worry about it. You're safe. I saved you.'

'No . . .' Suddenly Mia broke away from Yuri and went running into the dark and the falling snow.

'Mia!' Yuri cried.

'Go after her,' Adelaide told him. 'And, Yuri, take good care of her.'

'Yes, ma'am,' he promised, and looked back at the Doctor one last time. Like he wanted to say something. Instead, he followed Mia into the snow-swirling darkness beyond the street lights at the end of the road.

Together, the Doctor and Adelaide watched him go. Just the two of them left now in the somehow magnified hush that always came with gently falling snow. He looked at her, his hands in his pockets, waiting for her to speak.

Adelaide didn't know what to say. Standing here with the Doctor, it was like an awkward couple at the end of a first date that had taken a turn neither one of them had expected.

She looked at the townhouse opposite where the TARDIS had materialised; a nice comfortable home with a glossy black door and the kind of elegant brass knocker without which any house like it just wouldn't be complete, although now everybody had video doorbells so they could greet their callers by phone from just about anywhere on the planet. Though not as far away as Mars.

'That's my house,' she said quietly.

'I told you I'd get you home,' he said confidently, but without bluster, bathing in his own triumph but disappointed and suspicious that she didn't celebrate it with him.

She regarded him, disbelieving. Not because he had been *able* to do it, despite all the incredible odds against them – the Flood, the disintegrating shelter of Bowie Base, the nuclear detonation, the gulf of space that separated them from home, and the diktat of Time, itself – but simply because he *had* done it.

'You saved us.'

'You're welcome.' He said it like it was a challenge.

Adelaide looked up into the falling snow. She had gone through so many strange things. Today, and through her life.

Once she had seen alien worlds in the sky above her, and a barbaric metal-cased creature that, for all she knew, may have murdered her parents but let her live because it understood her future. And that future had been to die so that her granddaughter would begin the most important adventure her species would ever undertake. Somehow, in the last hundred seconds of Bowie Base One, that as-yet unlived history – the history-future this man had explained to her – all made sense. But now . . .

Now, what?

The Doctor's voice came to her through the falling snow. 'Your daughter, you'll see her again. And your granddaughter – little Suzie – you'll finally meet her. Get to hold her. You wanted to do that, didn't you?'

She looked at him. 'But I'm supposed to be dead!'

'Not anymore.'

It was a proclamation. A two-word blunt instrument that he wielded without apology.

She looked at him and remembered the man she had met on Mars only a few hours before. She remembered his eyes, how they had sparkled with an energetic joy, and yet she had seen pain and sorrow in them, too. These eyes were different; they burned with a belligerent defiance. She had come to trust him in the short time she had known him; now she realised that trust had gone, swept away by a wave of confusion and something close to fear.

'Suzie, my granddaughter. The person she was meant to become – it might never happen now. You said I had to die in order for that to happen, for her to take humanity into deep space. You've changed all that.'

The Doctor shrugged dismissively and drew a line in the snow with the rubber toe of his trainer. 'Naah,' he said. 'Captain Adelaide can inspire her in person. Details have changed but the story's the same.'

He had got her angry now, going back on everything he had told her at Bowie, rewriting her future and her granddaughter's fate on a whim. 'You can't *know* that!' she countered. 'You've changed things. You've *disrupted* them! Now, if my family changes, then the whole of history could change. The future of the human race! No one should have that much power!'

The Doctor stared back at her. 'Tough.'

Adelaide stepped back, away from him, afraid of him.

He watched her, a silent statue with snow gathering on his shoulders and in his hair.

'You should have left us there.'

I tried, thought the Doctor, *and I couldn't do it. Can't she see that?*

Adelaide had pleaded with him as he stood in the Bowie Base airlock: 'Help me.' And it had torn him apart to walk away from her, to leave her to her inevitable death. Didn't she see that he had saved her because she – Adelaide Brooke, who was meant to inspire a new age for humanity – had given him the strength to finally understand his place in the entire universe?

He shook his head, trying to find the words so that she could understand that he had a handle on things, and that it was all OK, that he was *the Doctor*.

'Adelaide, I've done this sort of thing before,' he said more calmly, 'in small ways.' There had been Pompeii, wartime London, soldiers across time abducted by the War Chief ... 'I've saved plenty of little people. But never anyone as important as you.' And suddenly he was celebrating again. 'Adelaide Brooke! Oh, I'm good!'

'Little people?' she gasped. 'What, like Yuri and Mia? Who decides whether or not people are important? You?'

He felt the rebuke like a slap across his face, but he wasn't about to accept it. There were things over the centuries that he had regretted. Saving Adelaide wasn't going to be one of them.

'Who do you think stopped the Daleks when they stole Earth?' he demanded. 'Who do you think put all those planets back where they should've been, and brought Earth back to the Solar System?'

Adelaide shrugged. 'You didn't save my parents and all the other people the Daleks exterminated.'

'Do you want me to? I could go back. Right now. Save John and Tessa. Happy families. How would you like that? I could. Just like that.'

He clicked his fingers. The sound was sharp and loud, like a gunshot.

Adelaide stared at him, her mind tumbling over itself in disbelief, *and belief*.

But he didn't go back into his blue box and travel to the night she had lost them; he began to walk towards her. 'You see, for a long time now I thought I was just a survivor – the last of my kind – but I'm not just a survivor, I'm a lot more than that. I'm the *winner*. That's who I am. The Time Lord Victorious!'

He stood over her, looking down into her eyes. Adelaide stared back.

'So, you can do whatever you want?'

'Oh, yes!'

'And there's no one to stop you?'

'No.'

She could see it in his eyes: it was the truth, simple and dangerous.

'This is wrong, Doctor. I don't care who you are. The Time Lord Victorious is wrong.'

'That's for me to decide,' he told her.

Adelaide knew that compared to him, she was just a child; not really much older than the small girl who had seen a Dalek from her bedroom window. She knew she could likely never grasp his decisions, his reasons, and could see that the Doctor had grown tired of trying to explain them to her.

'It's time you went home,' he said. Behind her the house stood in darkness, the heavy curtains drawn, snow collecting on the windowsills and the steps up to the door. 'All locked up. You've been away. Still, that's easy.'

He drew the thing he called his screwdriver from his pocket and aimed it at the townhouse. She heard it make a brief low noise, and saw her front door spring open. Again, he aimed it at the first floor and a light came on in there. Satisfied with himself, he restored the gadget to his coat.

'All yours.'

She looked from the house back to the Doctor. 'Is there anything you can't do?'

'Not anymore.'

And she saw it was true.

Adelaide turned away from him and walked towards her house.

The Doctor stood in the snow and watched her go.

He doubted that she would ever understand. She would ponder it throughout her life, he knew. All the people he had met during his travels through time and space must feel his presence in their lives long after he had gone. Even those, he thought sadly, who could no longer remember him. He remained there with them like a phantom caught out of the corner of their eye; not there but there. But he had touched Adelaide Brooke more deeply, more fundamentally, than most. He had saved her from Time itself. And she would never grasp why; a human lifespan was simply too short, its existence and experience too restricted.

The Doctor watched as Adelaide walked up the steps to the shiny black front door that she'd thought she would never see again. He had brought Adelaide home and, however confused about it she might feel, it made him smile.

He stood in the silent street and the snow fell from

the dark above him. He thought of the prophecy he'd been told by the woman on the bus.

It is returning through the dark.

Well, let it come, he thought.

Finally, he knew who he was.

The Time Lord Victorious.

He was the saviour of worlds. The master of destinies. Time and space were his. He could do with them what he would. There was no one that could challenge him. No one that could stop him. He had thought he was the Last of the Time Lords, but he was much, much more.

He was the Time Lord Victorious.

Adelaide went through the front door and closed it behind her. The Doctor turned to face his TARDIS.

He almost missed the flash of blue light. He caught it in his peripheral vision. A pulse of bright electric blue that spilt through the drawn curtains in the downstairs windows of Adelaide's house.

And sent him falling to his knees in the snow outside the TARDIS. As if he had been thrown to the ground as Time itself had shuddered.

Chapter 19

The Song in the Snow

The Doctor was on his knees in the snow. He could feel his back against the TARDIS. Its door was closed, and he didn't remember shutting it. He was sure it had stood open as Yuri and Mia had left. He felt the wet snow soaking into his body. He was shivering.

His mind was replaying the last few seconds before he had fallen, showing him details his consciousness had missed as he had turned back to the TARDIS and left Adelaide to the new life he had given her.

Her head had been bowed as she approached her open door. He saw it now; they were the measured deliberate steps of a woman making a grave decision. She had paused in the doorway of her house and had looked back at him. He had been too consumed with his own achievement, his subjugation of Time, to notice as he had turned back to his TARDIS, ready to challenge the end that was coming towards him through the dark. He was the Time Lord Victorious. Time was no longer the master of his destiny. There were no fixed points. He had travelled Time for centuries, but now he had *conquered* it. Time was his dominium and whatever his destiny was to be, it would be decided by him. Just as he had decided that of Adelaide Brooke.

He hadn't seen her eyes on him that final time, and he hadn't seen her hand reaching for the pulse pistol at her side as she had closed the door.

The Doctor shut his eyes and felt warm dampness on his cheeks that he knew had nothing to do with snow. His imagination had taken over from his subconscious memory as he saw Adelaide alone in her darkened house put the pistol to her head, courageously determined to put right what he had undertaken.

A single flash of blinding blue energy.

The date of Adelaide Brooke's death would still be recorded in the newspapers and history books as Friday November 21st 2059.

But mystery and conspiracy theories would orbit her death for years.

How had her body been found in her home with a fatal energy pulse wound when she should have died in the nuclear blast that destroyed Bowie Base One?

Was there ever really a Bowie Base One?

Had the entire endeavour been an elaborate hoax intended to distract Earth's troubled population from its twenty-first-century nightmares, and give it some hope in humanity's future?

Testimony by Yuri Kerenski and Mia Bennett before the Space Agency's official inquiry would tell the story as it had happened: how their crewmates had been taken by the Flood and how they had been rescued by a strange man – with a blue box that was bigger on the inside than the outside – who called himself the Doctor. Truth be told, the couple would be surprised by how easily the authorities accepted their detailing of their last day on Mars. But, of course, the Agency wasn't entirely unfamiliar with stories of the man UNIT had once counted as one of their own.

The inquiry would be held behind closed doors, little of it officially released – although carefully controlled leaks would seep onto the internet over time. Adelaide's daughter, Emily, would be refused access to the inquiry, but would seek out Yuri and Mia and hear everything from them as Suzie Fontana-Brooke played with building blocks on the floor nearby. Everything from when the Doctor had been found on the Martian surface to the moment they had left him with her mother on that snow-laden street outside Adelaide's house.

But why, after surviving the horrors they encountered on Mars, Captain Adelaide had chosen to take her own life was as much a mystery for them as everyone else. Whatever her reasons, she had been a hero without whom none of them would have survived. But she had not only saved them, she had saved Earth.

Three years later, when Yuri and Mia had their first child, they called her Adelaide.

Suzie grew up amid confused public views of her grandmother. There were those who believed the conspiracy theories that Bowie Base One had never really existed; there were others who had read information leaked from the inquiry who saw her as a legendary pioneer. When Suzie was ten, Emily played her the recording she had made of her conversation with Yuri and Mia, always intending to share it with her daughter when she was old enough to understand it without fear of its horrors. 'After all, you're practically an adult,' Emily said. But Suzie had never believed the conspiracy theories; to her, Adelaide had always been a hero, a legend. The recording would only confirm that.

Seventeen years later, Suzie Fontana-Brooke would fulfil her grandmother's legacy at the controls of *Lightspeed Alpha*, the ship that would for the first time take humanity to the stars.

The Doctor understood. Adelaide Brooke had killed herself to correct the damage he had done. He saw it now and, as the snow came down, he cried.

'*I don't care who you are. The Time Lord Victorious is wrong.*'

Even a Time Lord – even the *last* Time Lord – had no business trying to control Time. Adelaide Brooke was the hero that he had read about in that newspaper on that wet day in New York. Even when he had taken that away from her, she had been heroic, with the courage to reset Time. Even in his shock and grief, he'd felt it lock back on course, like a train that had momentarily jumped its tracks but then miraculously found them again.

The TARDIS had felt it too; it had slammed its door on him and his arrogant meddling.

The Doctor sobbed because he knew that he had gone too far. That Time, with all its wonderful and dark complexities and unfathomable twists was his master. And whatever was coming for him through the darkness was unstoppable.

He heard singing.

It was a song he had heard before, far, far away and both long ago and in the distant, distant future. It was a beautiful wordless song that soared and dipped, it was the song of the Ood and it was their song for him.

He opened his eyes and saw a figure standing on the other side of the street, snow swirling around its slight body.

Ood Sigma.

Clinging to the TARDIS for support, the Doctor climbed to his feet and tried to find his voice.

The Ood song filled the otherwise silent snow-laden night. Ood Sigma watched him, unmoving, untouched by the snow, the sphere that translated his telepathic song for the Doctor to hear, glowing gently in his hand.

'Is this it?' the Doctor cried out. 'Is this my death?' Perhaps after everything he had done, he deserved it.

The Ood said nothing.

The Doctor heard his song rise high and for a moment Ood Sigma was obscured by a flurry of snow. The song melted into the night air and, if he had ever been there, Ood Sigma had gone. The Doctor was left, cold and alone, with the knowledge of what he had done, and the knowledge of what was soon to come.

His hands were frozen as he fumbled the small silver key from his pocket and opened the TARDIS door again.

Inside, he closed the door behind him, leaning on it, feeling the warmth of his ship, though his hearts remained chilled.

'Your song is ending,' Carmen had said. 'It is returning through the dark. He will knock four times.'

And the Doctor had seen the darkness.

He moved away from the door and shrugged off the overcoat as he reached the TARDIS console. With long-practised movements he primed the ancient engines. The rotor at the heart of the controls began to rise and sink, and the TARDIS engines roared.

No one saw the police box vanish from the street, and the imprint it left in the snow, and the footprints of those who had left it, were soon covered by fresh flurries, as if none of what had taken place there had ever happened.

At the console, the Doctor stood in silence as the TARDIS travelled through the Time Vortex. The understanding of what he had tried to do, what he had tried to become, now chilled him like the melting snow in his hair that now dripped down his spine.

In the hush of the TARDIS, he said, 'No!'

The Doctor had seen the darkness, but he was determined that he would not let it take him.

Acknowledgements

It's been a treat to return to Mars and relive the fixed point in time that is Bowie Base One. The script, of course, was co-written with the creative Godzilla that is Russell T Davies, with whom, as always, it was a joyous education to work.

This was the second stab at what was originally intended to be a Christmas episode. The first concept had seen an Earth where everybody vanished on Christmas Eve but for one woman (who was a lot like Adelaide), who had been looking forward to spending it with her family. Then the Doctor showed up and, soon after, a whole cavalcade of weird aliens. But Russell thought the idea was a bit swords-and-sorcery, so we met up in Cardiff Bay and he talked about how he wanted to do something near-future on Mars.

NASA had just announced that its Phoenix Mars Lander had found ice in the Martian soil and 'The Waters of Mars' wrote its own title.

I wanted it to be scary. I loved the idea of drowned

zombies. But over development it was Russell who added the Doctor's existential battle with Time, and the Time Lord Victorious. I've always marvelled that however scary the Flood might have been, in 'The Waters of Mars', it is the Doctor himself that makes the story truly terrifying. And that – along with David Tennant's performance and Graeme Harper's direction – is what makes it such a great episode to have worked on.

So, my thanks to Julie Gardner for inviting me to the party, to Russell for making it so much fun, and to my script editor at the time, Gary Russell, who in preparation for this book, fourteen years later, was still able to provide me with valuable advice and every draft of 'The Waters of Mars' script!